PENGUIN

Twins

Chris Gregory was born in Mount Gambier in 1970.
He has written extensively for anthologies and journals.
Twins is his first book.

Chris Gregory

PENGUIN BOOKS

Penguin Books Australia Ltd
487 Maroondah Highway, PO Box 257
Ringwood, Victoria 3134, Australia
Penguin Books Ltd
Harmondsworth, Middlesex, England
Viking Penguin, A Division of Penguin Books USA Inc.
375 Hudson Street, New York, New York 10014, USA
Penguin Books Canada Limited
10 Alcorn Avenue, Toronto, Ontario, Canada M4V 3B2
Penguin Books (N.Z.) Ltd
Cnr Rosedale and Airborne Roads, Albany, Auckland, New Zealand

First published by Penguin Books Australia Ltd 1997

10 9 8 7 6 5 4 3 2 1

Copyright © Chris Gregory, 1997

All rights reserved. Without limiting the rights under copyright reserved above, no part of this publication may be reproduced, stored in or introduced into a retrieval system, or transmitted, in any form or by any means (electronic, mechanical, photocopying, recording or otherwise), without the prior written permission of both the copyright owner and the above publisher of this book.

Design by Peter Hennessey, Drome Pty Ltd
Printed and bound in Australia by Australian Print Group, Maryborough

National Library of Australia
Cataloguing-in-Publication data

Gregory, Chris, 1970–.
  Twins.
  ISBN 014 025604 0.
  I. Title.
A823.3

Contents

List of illustrations	xii
Twins	1
Mabel Ambrose's Head	8
The 5000 Fingers of Doctor T	38
Mock Chicken	58
The Finger Game	68
Since the Accident	80
Teratology	108
Stucco	122
Powerhouse	136
Tintooki Frogs	164
Salaryman	176
Bring Me the Head of Dora Kent	210
Jackie Chan	228
References	267
The Raymond Scott Archive	270

For my father, Max

Acknowledgements

First of all, I would like to thank the people in the writing business who have encouraged me: Gerald Murnane, as good a teacher as a writer could have; Elizabeth Flann; Carmel Bird; John Hanrahan; Helen Daniel; George Papaellinas; Paul and Gary at Polyester Books; and Des and Jurate at the Greville Street Bookstore.

I would like to thank Sandy Webster, who first approached me about signing with Penguin and showed confidence in my abilities; Bryony Cosgrove, who has treated me with more respect and leniency than any author could expect from a publisher; and Foong Ling Kong, my twin, my friend, my editor and fellow fan of Frank Sinatra.

I would also like to thank all the friends who have contributed so much to my work: Peter Hennessey, whose virtuoso design hardly indicates the depth of his involvement with this book, let alone the level of his friendship; Patricia Piccinini, for her illustrations and long-standing friendship and influence since I had barely begun to write; Mark Dundon for his beautifully poetic photographs and his sinister, Chandler-esque influence, especially regarding the subject of chicken processing plants; Chris Langton, for sharing with me a love/hate relationship with cuteness; Louise Wilson for finding the letter I used in the story 'Teratology' and then thinking that I would think it was funny enough to give to me, as well as her kindness and support; Dennis Daniel, for allowing me to re-tell his Jackie Chan story, to photograph him for my 'Jackie Chan' story, and for his exceptional friendliness and assistance; Helen Stuckey, for similar chores, particularly those involving bodies described as cities and cities described as bodies; Rohan Storey, for giving his time to list the buildings in Melbourne which I call 'copies' and he calls 'tributes'; Mark Gregory, for his well-intentioned advice; Shiralee Saul, who has consistently said nice things about me behind my back; John Bleaney, The World's Greatest Artist™, who let me rip off one of his ideas for the cover of this book and who has always been prepared to stop work and drink himself stupid with me, at any time of the day, no matter how much work he has to do, whenever I decide to turn up unannounced at the Continental Cafe on Greville Street, Prahran; Irwin Chusid, whom I have never met in person, but who made the story 'Powerhouse' possible; Peter Wolcott, for allowing me to interview him about his involvement with the fall of Skylab and the subsequent Miss Universe weirdness; Sarah Atkinson for well-timed support; Miranda Letcher, whom I have often thought about; Richard Adamson, for defrosting my refrigerator; and especially Kirky, for giving me an appreciation of food and of food technology, among many other things, and for living with and putting up with me for more than six years.

I blame all of these people for this book, and for my happiness.

Some of these stories have been previously published in the anthologies *Picador New Writing 2*, *Hot Type*, *Hot Sand*, and *Red Hot Notes*, and the literary magazines *RePublica* and *Overland*.

List of Illustrations

Cover, illustration by Chris Gregory.

Page xiv, photograph by Peter Hennessey.

Page 8, 'Exhibit A: Design for a tattoo', Patricia Piccinini.

Page 15, 'Exhibit B: Lateral section through right eye (lateral aspect)', Patricia Piccinini.

Page 21, 'Exhibit C: Transverse section through neck (distal aspect)', Patricia Piccinini.

Page 24, 'Exhibit D: Standard autopsy suturing (sample)', Patricia Piccinini.

Page 25, 'Exhibit E: Embroidered Monograph (sample: M)', Patricia Piccinini.

Page 31, 'Exhibit F: Morphology of breast (proximal aspect, skin removed)', Patricia Piccinini.

Page 33, 'Ornamental boss or metope (Neo-classical)', Patricia Piccinini.

Pages 38, 43, 47, 51, 55, photographs by Peter Hennessey.

Page 58, photograph by Mark Dundon.

Page 68, illustration by Peter Hennessey.

Page 80, Moon rock, Smithsonian Institution, Washington, DC, USA, photograph by Peter Hennessey.

Page 85, Industrial space heater, photograph by Mark Dundon.

Page 89, Braun coffee machine, photograph by Mark Dundon.

Page 93, Electronic componentry, photograph by Mark Dundon.

Page 97, Remote control, photograph by Mark Dundon.

Page 103, Transformer, photograph by Mark Dundon.

Pages 108, 115, 119 from the series 'Teratologies', Patricia
   Piccinini, 1994. Photograph by Mark Dundon.
Page 122, illustration by Dennis Daniel.
Pages 136, 140, 143, 147, 149, 153, 155, 159, 161,
   photographs courtesy Raymond Scott archive.
Page 164, The Chicken Holocaust, from a photograph
   by Chris Gregory.
Pages 176, 181, 191, 203, photographs by Mark Dundon.
Page 210, photograph by Patricia Piccinini.
Page 217, Adventure golf, Pigeon Forge, TN, USA,
   photograph by Peter Hennessey.
Page 221, Liberace Museum, Las Vegas, NV, USA,
   photograph by Peter Hennessey.
Page 225, Niagara Falls Motel, Niagara Falls, TN, USA,
   photograph by Peter Hennessey.
Page 228, illustration by Peter Hennessey.
Page 233, Shot tower, Melbourne Central, photograph by Peter
   Hennessey.
Page 237, Dennis Daniel with Jackie Chan's autograph,
   photograph by Peter Hennessey.
Page 245, The world's largest imitation Seiko fob-watch,
   Melbourne Central, photograph by Peter Hennessey.
Page 249, The 'Paris End' of Collins Street, Melbourne,
   photograph by Peter Hennessey.
Page 257, The 'Duomo' of the Exhibition Buildings, Melbourne,
   photograph by Peter Hennessey.

TWINS

I hope you appreciate me taking the time to tell you this. I live in a two-bedroom flat in an inner suburb of Melbourne. The two of us live here. The rent is reasonable, but in recent months we have started to run out of space. During the past eighteen months I started to earn an adult wage, even more than an adult wage, for the first time in my life. I spent most of the money I made on *consumer electronics*, then food, musical recordings and books, in that order. The Sony Centre even sent me a twenty-dollar gift voucher for my birthday this year, for being such a good customer. Before I started earning an adult wage I spent most of my money on rent and then food, and the food was of nowhere near as much variety or of as good a quality as the food I eat now.

All of the consumer electronics I bought take up a certain amount of room, but the real problem has been finding somewhere to put the boxes that all these things came in. I could throw out the boxes, but the resale value of these sorts of items – televisions and video recorders and laser disc players and stereo components – is higher if the original boxes they were shipped in have been kept, and having the original boxes to put them in makes moving house easier. Being forced to move because my home is full of boxes seems stupid, but I have yet to make up my mind about what I should do.

I use one of the bedrooms as my office, which is where I write and work. I spend most of my time there, but after a few hours of sitting there on my own I sometimes get cabin fever and go wandering.

An old Italian man with a three-legged German Shepherd hangs around outside of his house on the corner of my street and the street that leads to the closest tram stop. As I approach him he waves to me and smiles, and as I get closer we exchange a few words. He usually asks: 'Off to work?' and I say: 'Kind of.'

I wait at the tram stop until a tram arrives and then I catch the tram in to the city. I hear a lot of things on the tram: the conversations of the poor and the stupid and the aged and the sick. I have thought about bringing a small tape recorder on the tram with me, to record the conversations I hear, but I don't and I forget them.

Someone once told me of the work of a psychologist, whose name I remember but doubt I could spell correctly, who compiled a list that he called *the hierarchy of needs*. The psychologist claimed that once a category at a lower level of the hierarchy had been satisfied, and only once the category had been satisfied, the individual would begin to perceive needs from the next level. The base level of the hierarchy was called the physiological level, and consisted of things like food and shelter and a relatively

constant body temperature. I cannot remember what was described on the higher levels. All I can say is that my own hierarchy of needs has not progressed beyond the acquisition of consumer electronics.

Perhaps some readers will find the idea of reading a book written by someone whose main preoccupations are with buildings and food to be slightly depressing. I can only reply by repeating Raymond Chandler's claim that most people would give up reading before they would give up coffee. And as far as the separate issue of taste goes, I can quite confidently say that, **after a short period of confusion,** I realised that my tastes had not significantly changed since I was nine years old.

I like to think of myself as a normal person. I feel pretty normal. If there was anything remarkable about me, I suppose I have read a hell of a lot of books. I pick things up easily. I can confidently hold a conversation with a funeral director or an electrical engineer or a musician or a liberal arts academic, although I am not saying I would necessarily want to.

I still read a lot, but very little of what I read is fiction. **The fiction I do read I have usually read before,** and some particular works I read compulsively over and over again. But my reading has purpose: I want to learn how one author creates a sense of unease from describing the furniture in a room, or how another author emulates the visual style of the old silent-movie comedians with words, or how another author constructs a world driven only by the demands of its own internal logic. I read fiction to understand how it works. I read fiction for the same reason a mechanic takes apart a motor or a medical student dissects a cadaver; but when I was a kid I read fiction for a very different reason, and I was a lot less discriminating.

When I was a kid I thought of the books I read as templates for my adult life. I thought that one day I would live the kind of life that was described in the books I had read, a life filled with meaningful and thought-provoking conversations and dramatic revelations about my own nature and the nature of others. I thought that the books I read offered me some insight into the way the world worked, showing me a faithful and accurate representation of the kind of existence I could expect to live in adulthood.

When I got older I had a lot of difficulty adjusting to the realities of the adult world. The world I discovered seemed like an inane parody of the world I had read about. Gradually I realised that the real world was flawed in ways that were not and could not be reproduced in a book of fiction. I learned that if I read a story a second time the outcome would be exactly the same: each time a character behaved in a certain way, the action would have the same result, and each action within the story followed the next with a certainty that the real world did not possess. A character in a book, I decided, was at worst a puppet, and at best, a component in a very specialised type of machine.

But for some reason I kept reading, and once I knew enough about how stories worked I started building them for myself. I could no longer pretend to understand what the nature of a thing was, or even what *nature* meant, but I knew that I could simulate its effects with a certain mechanical precision.

I was on a train some time ago, heading for the city. I cannot remember where I was travelling from, or what I had been doing there. On the seat behind me I heard two people talking.

'Listen to yourself. You talk and talk and it's all crap. It's completely meaningless. You talk for the sake of talking. You talk to hear the sound of your own voice, that's all.'

The other person took no offence at these words. They kept talking, imitating people they knew, discussing trivial plans and criticising each other in terms that most people would find extremely upsetting, as if each was trying to provoke an act of violence from the other. I felt tense listening to them, half expecting to get hit accidentally when the baiting turned into a fight. But the two people kept talking, and their voices maintained a casual, conversational tone.

When the train reached the city and stopped I stood up and turned around to look at them. They were twins, identical twins of **roughly my age,** with close-cropped hair and wearing denim jackets and jeans. I waited until they left the train and followed them up the escalator to the station. I was trying to get up the courage to approach them.

I wanted to tell them that I was a writer and that I was very interested in twins. This was not true at the time. I had met twins before, I even had friends with twin brothers or sisters, but I had never given this condition much thought. I had never listened to a pair of twins talk to each other before. In retrospect I wish I had approached them, but at the time the embarrassment that tapping one of them on the shoulder could have caused me seemed too much, and I lost them in the crowd of other people, normal people like me.

I am telling you this because it was the moment I realised that twins were the only people who really talked to each other like characters talked to each other in books.

Exhibit A: Design for a tattoo.

MABEL AMBROSE'S HEAD

It is Saturday, the 17th of December 1898. Francis James Logan boards the Glen Waverley train at Kooyong station, going to the city. Francis is twelve and a student at St Kevin's. He is a Young Liberal, an army cadet, and an avid rower. His father, once himself a student at St Kevin's, is in real estate. His mother has just completed the third year of a photography course at La Trobe University and was interviewed by *A Current Affair* at last year's Melbourne Cup. When asked if, given the harsh economic climate, some people might consider spending five thousand dollars on a hat 'obscene', she replied: 'Oh, no. Not at all. I think they enjoy it. It gives them an escape. It caters to their need for fantasy.'

At Heyington station some of Francis's school friends board the train, and as soon as the boys are in a group they become boisterous. I often see schoolboys on the Glen Waverley train engaged in *slant baiting* – harassing an isolated, and usually elderly, Asian passenger. If none is available they threaten the nearest senior citizen. Passengers who can defend themselves are always spared any direct harassment, although as I leave the train at East Richmond I have often been spat on from the open window of the departing train and had detritus thrown at me (usually, for some reason, apples. I imagine some parent, reading this, will be shocked to hear that their children are wasting their lunches).

The boys disembark at Flinders Street station, jostling each other as they walk to the St Kevin's boat shed. Francis, his younger brother Fred, and another boy (whose name does not appear in the police records) take out a flat-bottomed boat and row upstream along the northern bank of the Yarra. Francis spends much of his free time patrolling the Yarra for dead bodies, animal or human, which he then reports to the police. Recently he was presented with a small government award for his services, along with a five-pound reward. Between the Church Street and South Yarra railway bridges Francis notices a large wooden box, painted in a conspicuous Day-Glo yellow (as the company literature states: 'the great thing about Day-Glo fluorescent colours is that you can't miss them'), floating among some rushes. The boys struggle to bring the box aboard but it is too heavy for them to lift (it is only when Constables Kelly and Withers arrive, summoned by Fred from South Richmond Police station, that the boys notice a large stone tied to the box). As Francis tugs at the iron ring riveted to one end of the water-soaked box, the plywood panel comes off and, like some upside-down jack-in-the-box, a pair of decomposing feet pop out. This is a moment the boys will treasure, a story to awe their friends. Perhaps in twenty years they will recount it to their children.

'Cool . . .' Fred says.
The boys laugh.

Facts: The improvised coffin is a shoe box, or more accurately a 'boot trunk', 83 cm long, 45 cm wide and 38 cm deep, used for transferring large quantities of shoes from factory to retailer. Melbourne at the time had many such factories, which makes the source of the box untraceable. (On the subject of shoes, I must recommend Rocco's of Station Street, Malvern. I buy all my shoes there; Rocco makes them to my specifications. His shop is one of Melbourne's best-kept secrets – he has no phone and he does not advertise. He is particularly popular among musicians; the trip to Rocco's is an established ritual for bands who visit Melbourne, including, so the rumours go, U2 and David Bowie.) The interior of the box has been rather amateurishly wallpapered, and inside the lid is written the name 'T.R. Atkins'. This lead will be followed up by the police but will turn out to be a dead end. (There is no 'T.R. Atkins'. **The name is a fiction,** the product of a young woman's matrimonial fantasies. Otherwise, I feel compelled to mention, all names used in this story are **true**.)

Next item. The stone tied to the box is yellow sandstone, which is not to be found along the bank of the Yarra where the body was found. The coroner correctly assumes that the stone was taken from the Toorak side of the Yarra; this would suggest that the body was deposited in the Yarra somewhere near Williams Road. The trunk is wrapped with everyday wire, of the type found on Hills Hoists around the world, and provides the police with no further clues.

The body is of a young woman, 150 cm tall and weighing 45 kg. Comparing the body's dimensions to those of the box, we can imagine the compressed state of the body and the rough handling it has received. The force required to fit the body into the box was so great that the eyes have been projected from their sockets and lie on the frontal bone (I am justifying my earlier use of the word 'pop'). A policeman laughs: 'They must have used a shoehorn!' He uses the word 'they' because he has already decided that the box was too heavy for someone to have carried it to the river bank alone. The close confinement has retarded the decay of the body proper – the head is a different matter. As anyone who has an interest in forensics can tell you, the body decays in as many ways as there are people. This particular woman has decayed head-first. The head is black and swollen, while the body is white and exhibits none of the usual swelling and distension (caused by, among other things, sulphur combining with methaemoglobin in the gut). Another policeman, present at the morgue during the pathologist's examination, comments: 'It looks like someone's sewn an Abo's head on her,' prompting giggles from his partner. Both are nervous: it is likely that this is the first time either of them has seen a wholly unclothed female body, alive or dead, at least not so clearly lit. In view of the actions later taken by the police, the young sergeant's statement may be considered prophetic.

The government pathologist ignores the policemen's chatter. He is a professional. Many years have passed since he was a mischievous anatomy student. A popular prank among such students is to put severed extremities in other people's lockers. As a friend told me (an anatomy major himself): 'There is no way I'd donate my body to science ...' In his report to the police the pathologist concludes that the woman died as a result of chloroform incorrectly administered in the course of an illegal abortion, which was not then carried out. The foetus is of two months' duration, and so cannot be classed as stillborn (which is defined as being of at least twenty weeks' duration or more than four hundred grams). It is therefore not entitled to its own death certificate. Instead, the coroner records the foetus on its mother's certificate as an 'antecedent cause', a decision made with no apparent irony. When the examination has ended a junior is left to close up the body, returning the brain and internal organs to their rightful cavities, but leaving the stomach for the chief pathologist to send to a government analyst for further inspection. The body is then stored, in case it may be required for identification purposes. This is all standard procedure.

The name of the person responsible for the subsequent police investigation is not a matter of public record. By the standards of the day, this may be considered odd. The omission cannot be due to any sense of propriety: at no time are accusations of bad taste made by the public regarding the way the case is handled. Perhaps, as I envisage it, the police did not wish the source of their inspiration to be revealed.

I speculate. A group of policemen sit in Chloe's bar. They gaze at the painting of Chloe herself, the most famous example of the Bourgeois Realism school of painting in Australia (a style that, to my dismay, is becoming popular again. Walk past any poster shop and you will be confronted by a flock of cutesy cherubs or a bevy of drowning Ophelias. Presumably these are bought and proudly exhibited by the same people who bought posters of rainbows and unicorns in the seventies to express their individuality, who now aspire to high art but suffer from *Fantasia*-damaged sensibilities and a Garfield-induced addiction to 'rounded cuteness'). Weeks have passed, and there has been no further evidence. No leads have yet been established, which is strange given the amount of media attention the case has received (a re-enactment has even been made for *Crime-Stoppers* and will be aired next week). The police have abandoned hope that the perpetrators of the crime will come forth. The only prospect is that someone, family or friend, can identify the body.

'You know,' one of them says, 'if we actually showed the body around, somebody might recognise her.'

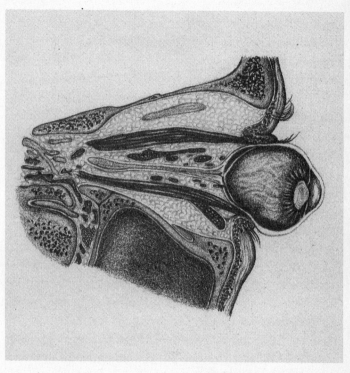

Exhibit B: Lateral section through right eye (lateral aspect).

'Jesus, you've seen it haven't you? The head is black. It's all puffed up. No-one's going to recognise that.'

The first cop swigs his Fosters. The atmosphere is oppressive. Above them the recently installed Optus billboard casts a cold corporate glow on passers-by. Seduced by the desire to impress the IBM set, Optus has neglected the public's need for friendly, warm personalities and cloying jingles. (I have a part-time job doing market research surveys. Never underestimate the power of the cloying jingle. When you think hot water systems you think Rheem and you probably know all the words to the song as well.)

Failure is a hard thing to face when you are drunk.

'Fuck it. Why the fuck not.'

The next day, hungover, the officers work out the practicalities of the plan. It would be difficult to cart the entire cadaver from place to place. They quickly decide that the torso is of little use for identification purposes, and would serve their plans best if severed from the item of interest. The head, that is.

Over the next few days, every policeman stationed in the metropolitan area is sent to Russell Street police headquarters. They queue to examine the artefact: a woman's head, sans body and interred in a large glass jar containing preserving spirits. When this fails to bear any useful information, the head is taken to Bourke Street GPO,

Mable Ambrose's Head

in the hope that an observant postman will recognise it. No success.

Disheartened, the head is returned home to the morgue. After a few days the police decide to present the abridged corpse to the public. **Some statistics:** in the three days from January 6 to 8 some two thousand people file past the head (this figure, as noted by the *Age*, 'does not include children, of whom there were many'). I assume that some approach with mixed feelings of anticipation and dread, fully expecting to recognise a loved one. Others experience less ambiguous emotions, enticed by the £250 reward being offered. The majority, however, are simply curious. As Alan Sharpe observes in his book *Crimes That Shocked Australia* (where I first came across this story), 'Had the police been permitted to charge an entrance fee to the thousands who came to stare at the head in the city morgue it would have swollen the coffers of the Victorian police benevolent fund beyond conception.' Such callous opportunism would, however, have been regarded as deplorable in those strait-laced Victorian times.

It is **January 11, 1899.** Robert Gabriel approaches the police on behalf of Thekla Dubberke, whom he has convinced to step forward to relieve her troubled conscience. She is sent for by the police and, once reassured that she may turn Queen's evidence, **reveals her story.** I have taken the liberty of dramatising certain scenes and dialogues. I believe this is an acceptable journalistic practice.

Miss Dubberke is 20, and was born in Berwick to the southwest of Melbourne. She began her career as a domestic servant, fell in with the wrong crowd, turned to prostitution, then landed a role on *Chances*. She played the mute and possibly retarded Imogen, daughter of an evil and hideously rich criminal mastermind who saw fit to clothe her exclusively in see-through negligees. One of the many highlights of her role was the dubious honour of being the first woman to give birth to a fruit bat on national television. In keeping with the character she portrayed, she has told me that she identifies 'profoundly' with Marilyn Monroe. At the age of thirteen she cut the name 'Marilyn' into her forearm in homage to the actress, although when she showed the scars to me I was unable to make them out. Like Marilyn, she plans to die young (at 25, if memory serves me), and I imagine that somewhere in the files of the *Truth* newspaper a story has already been written with the headline:

CHANCES STAR BIZARRE SUICIDE

MARILYN DEATH PACT

Underneath it is a photograph of her in one of the negligees mentioned above, with the caption: *She was obsessed with Marilyn Monroe.*

When *Chances* is axed by Channel Nine, Thekla finds herself at a loose end (although it is rumoured that Kerry Packer influenced the decision, I feel that poor ratings were the deciding factor. However, it is quite possible that after the *Australia's Naughtiest Home Videos* incident, an executive took this as a precedent – Packer's way of saying that he wanted to clean up Channel Nine's image – and acted accordingly). She takes employ and lodgings with Madame Olga Radalyski, a palm reader and crystal ball reader, while maintaining a discreet and high-paying clientele on the side. I was disappointed to find that 73 Osborne Street, South Yarra, no longer existed – Madame Olga's cottage has been torn down and a block of flats built in its place. There is no longer a 73 Osborne Street, the flats taking up the space of two of the original houses. I had planned to interview the present occupants and confront them with the sordid tale relating to their home. The reaction to my invading and disrupting the ambience and tasteful tranquillity of the tree-lined street would have made good reading; unfortunately, it was not to be.

Thekla is engaged by Madame Olga as a domestic servant, and serves as an assistant to Madame Olga in her dual occupations – fortune teller and abortionist. To set the scene (a stock one, I give you that), we will eavesdrop on Madame Olga. She sits, appropriately garbed, at a round table with a crystal ball at its centre. The customer (perhaps yourself, dear reader) sits opposite her.　　　　She takes

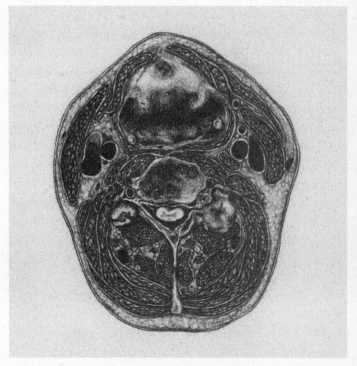

Exhibit C: Transverse section through neck (distal aspect).

your hand and, to demonstrate her ability, reveals to you just what kind of person you really are:

Some of your aspirations tend to be pretty unrealistic. At times you are extroverted, affable, sociable, while at other times you are introverted, weary and reserved. You have found it unwise to be too frank in revealing yourself to others. You pride yourself on being an independent thinker and do not accept others' opinions without satisfactory proof. You prefer a certain amount of change and variety, and become dissatisfied when hemmed in by restrictions and limitations. At times you have serious doubts as to whether you have made the right decision or done the right thing. Disciplined and controlled on the outside, you tend to be worrisome and insecure on the inside. While you have some personality weaknesses, you are generally able to compensate for them. You have a great deal of unused capacity which you have not turned to your advantage. You have a tendency to be critical of yourself. You have a strong need for other people to like you and for them to admire you.

This spiel was first used in 1948 by Bertram Forer in a classroom demonstration of 'cold reading' – I found it in a book by Douglas Hofstadter called *Metamagical Themas*. Forer's students, who thought the sketch was uniquely intended for them as a result of a personality test, gave the sketch an average rating of 4.26 on a scale of 0 (poor) to 5 (perfect). Everybody sees themselves like this – it is unlikely that any sane individual would believe the reverse of any of these statements was true about them. On top of that, you have paid for the service: hardly anyone can admit to having been swindled.

This is, at any rate, only a front for the more lucrative abortion business. I was told by an officer at the police museum that this was a common combination of careers at the time. As the neighbours later attested, the screams that they frequently heard coming from the house would have been hard to ignore if Madame Olga was a practitioner of a less esoteric art.

Enter Mabel Ambrose. Poor Mabel has got herself knocked up by a Prahran real estate agent, Travice Alexander Tod. Travice, who was previously acquainted with Olga (and presumably in the same capacity), turns to her for help. Madame Olga agrees, and to facilitate the operation Mabel moves in with her. I imagine this period to be a pleasant interlude in Mabel's previously miserable proletarian existence; Olga relieves her worries and apprehensions, reassures and comforts her. Besides, Olga is amusingly eccentric, old before her time and deaf as a post, using an ear trumpet that one must shout in to be heard. Conversations with Olga tend to be a bit one-sided; Mabel, relieved of even this obligation, is silent as Olga speaks:

'You know, Mabel, it is the best thing for you to get rid of the child. I mean look at the world today, with the hole in the ozone layer and the greenhouse effect and the depletion of the world's resources. Kids these days have no respect, no respect for tradition, no respect for their elders. And the music they listen to,

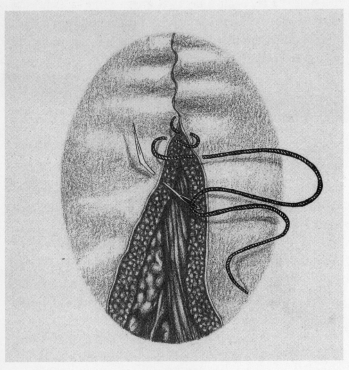

Exhibit D: Standard autopsy suturing (sample).

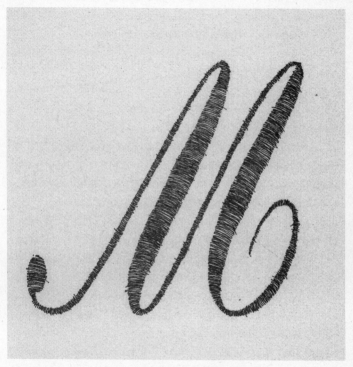

Exhibit E: Embroidered Monograph (sample: M).

no feeling, no soul, not like the Beatles or Janis or The Doors, now that was music . . . and the clothes they wear are so stupid. Do you know how much sneakers cost? Don't they realise how stupid they look? Believe me, you don't want to find yourself forking out three hundred bucks for some lousy fluoro footwear do you?'

After this they watch *River's Edge* on video.

The first attempted abortion is unsuccessful; no details of the attempt or of the nature of the difficulty are to be found in the police records. Suffice it to say that Madame Olga's usual techniques fail to work. Olga, unsure of what to do, calls a highly placed Collins Street doctor, Doctor William Henry Gaze, for advice. He is a friend of Olga's, and on occasion has made use of Thekla's services. He suggests to Olga the use of chloroform. Olga sends Thekla to visit a Mr Edward Fisher, who is the dispenser at the Alfred Hospital. (Fisher, as it later turned out, was acquainted with Thekla in a 'professional capacity'. During the trial it is revealed that Thekla and Fisher had engaged in 'lecherous behaviour' on several occasions in the hospital dispensary, in itself a scene worthy of *Chances*.) Fisher supplies the chloroform that is to kill Mabel Ambrose, although the charges against him at the inquest are dropped for lack of evidence.

Two screams are heard coming from Mabel's bedroom. Thekla rushes in to find Mabel on the floor unconscious; a spray of foam and blood spurts from between her bruised lips. Olga tells Thekla to go to the corner hotel to fetch some brandy to revive her. When she returns Mabel is dead, and Olga drinks the brandy herself.

Olga calls Dr Gaze, the man who had recommended the use of chloroform for the abortion. She tells him that Mabel is seriously ill. When he arrives and sees the dead body Olga demands that he make out a death certificate. He flatly refuses and rushes from the house, despite Olga's pleading. It is this decision that saves him at the trial.

Mabel's boyfriend, Travice, is less than pleased. The news reaches him via his slim-line Motorola (a mighty three inches – bear in mind that the size of the cellular phone is inversely proportional to the owner's penis length), as he does lunch with the new office girl ('an office tradition', he tells her) at the Trattoria on Toorak Road.

'It's my stockbroker. I'll just be a minute . . .' and he blows her a kiss as he stands, adjusts his floral tie (which is another penis. I always laugh when a television host, intimidated by a difficult guest, nervously fiddles with his tie, oblivious to the symbolic nature of the act), and retreats to the security of his navy BMW. (A womb. Also note: the navy blue BMW is the automobile of choice for real estate agents. Another piece of useful information.) To continue the conversation:

'Are you sure she's dead? . . . and he refused to sign the death certificate . . . Jesus, are you sure he won't talk . . . yeah, okay. Look, I know what to do. Take off all her clothes and burn them, burn all her stuff. Then you'll have to put her in something and load it down with stones . . . you got that? I'll be over as soon as I can.'

Travice returns to his meal of lamb vignettes, looking glum.

'What's wrong?' She lays her hand on his, sensing an opportunity.

He puts on a brave smile. 'Just a bad investment.'

She pouts sympathetically.

The writer finds that he has encountered a difficulty. The reader surely is interested in the eventual fate of Thekla Dubberke, Travice Alexander Tod and Madame Olga. If not, the writer has failed. Given the material he has access to (police records, newspaper clippings and so on), and the obscurity of the case, this information is not available. It would be tempting to write: Travice Tod died at thirty-six from a brain tumour. His widow attempted to sue Motorola but was not successful, due to the lack of real evidence that mobile phones cause cancer. However, the writer feels that he could not write this. He has tried to stick to **the facts.** He has, as far as possible, included **only the truth:** things that he has either read or seen for himself. Where that has not been possible he has made it very clear that he is speculating. **It is not the writer's intention to produce a work of fiction.**

It is the evening of December 14, 1898. Travice leaves his BMW at work (432 Chapel Street, now Ensign Crash Repairs), and catches the tram to Mr Alfred's livery stable in Windsor. He hires a dog cart, which he rides to Madame Olga's house. Thekla helps Travice move the trunk from Olga's living room, and they load it on the cart. (I will take this opportunity to reveal the ownership of the box. It is Thekla's. It was to be used as a glory box in readiness for her forthcoming marriage to a Mr Atkins. In a sentimental moment she had written inside the lid her own initials alongside the name of her husband-to-be. Hence the name 'T.R. Atkins' that I mentioned earlier.)

When it is dark, Thekla and Travice trot down Chapel Street to Williams Road, Toorak, above the Church Street bridge. During a lull in the traffic, the pair carry the box to the river bank. Thekla stays with the trunk while Travice scouts around. He sees a young couple embracing in some bushes – he panics. He returns to Thekla and they leave the box where it is and go back to Olga's.

The three of them wait: Thekla and Travice and

Olga. They play cards. They drink wine. They talk a little. Steve Vizard interviews Julian Clary, who makes comments about his sex life. Steve fiddles with his tie. Travice tells the story about Jennifer Keyte and Johnny Diesel but they have all heard it before.

They switch to Channel Ten. They watch a movie, *The Thing With Two Heads*. Ray Milland plays a racist brain surgeon with terminal cancer. He arranges to have his head transplanted on to the healthy body of a volunteer convict from death row (Rosey Grier). When he awakens from the operation he discovers, to his horror, they have grafted his head on to a black man's body. The plan is that once Ray Milland's head has fully healed they will amputate Grier's head. Until then they must share the one body. Grier, who still controls the body, escapes with the assistance of a black doctor who is fed up with Milland's racism. Grier must prove his innocence before he is recaptured.

Thekla and Travice leave during the motorcycle chase. It is one o'clock. They go back and slide the box into the Yarra.

Olga watches until the end of the movie. In the final scene we see Milland's severed head connected to a life support machine in the operating room. It speaks.

'Get . . . me . . . another . . . body!'

Fade to credits.

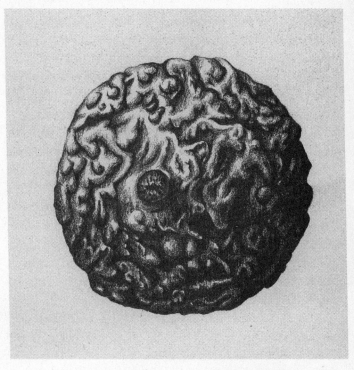

Exhibit F: Morphology of breast (proximal aspect, skin removed).

Robert Gabriel is, I suppose, the hero of this story; unfortunately, police records are not often concerned with the personal details of the innocent. The information available is too sketchy for me to attempt any real characterisation. If this was a more traditional work, I would have been tempted to cast him as an altruistic young man, acting purely out of a concern for justice. I think that if he had refused the reward money I would have cast him thus. He did not refuse the money. So, the facts:

Robert Gabriel is twenty. He works in his mother's chemical firm, which is located in the same building as Travice Tod's real estate agency. He tells the police that Madame Olga has asked him to obtain illegal drugs for her on several occasions. Presumably, he refused.

Robert knew Mabel Ambrose from her frequent visits to Travice in the estate agency. When the body is first discovered in the Yarra he jokingly asks Travice if it is Mabel. Travice replies, say the records, with a comment 'of an extremely callous nature'. I presume that to mean that he tells Robert to fuck off.

Robert does not give up, however. When he later mentions to Travice that he hasn't seen Mabel for some time, he is told she has gone to South Australia. This does not strike Robert as a reasonable explanation. I think it fair to say that Robert is a persistent character, and fairly suspicious by nature. When the head is put on display he goes to the morgue and sees it but is not able to recognise it as Mabel.

Now there is a gap. Somehow Robert gets to know Thekla, and she unburdens herself to him. He

Exhibit G: Ornamental boss or metope (Neo-classical).

offers to go to the police for her, and the circle is closed. The story is complete. As to how Robert knows Thekla or even Madame Olga, I cannot say. It was not recorded anywhere, as far as I can tell. Perhaps the police had uncovered enough truth for a conviction and left it at that, as in a Dashiell Hammett novel. I would imagine that any dealings between Olga and Travice would be conducted surreptitiously, and certainly not at Travice's place of work. Abortion was, after all, a capital offence. How then did Robert meet Thekla? It seems likely to me that Robert knew more and was more involved than was revealed. To start with, I see no reason for Robert to have been so suspicious – it does not ring true to me. I cannot really say. I am unable to piece together the relationships between the characters, which is a shortcoming of my material.

One reason I chose to tell this story was that it happened not so long ago that the world it describes is alien, but just long enough ago that no-one can remember it. It exists on the edge of experience. I once read that a lifetime lasts for three generations: the knowledge of the grandparent is passed to the parent is passed to the child. This means that an individual can at best have access to a hundred years of lived experience. 1898 is gone from us. There is nobody left to tell us what it was really like. 'For now we see as through a mirror darkly; but then face to face; now I know in part; but then shall I know even as also I am known.' That's from Shakespeare.

The trial of Olga Radalyski, Travice Tod and Dr William Gaze takes place at the Central Criminal Court before Chief Justice Sir John Madden on February 22, 1899. It lasts for four days, and scores of people are turned away from the overflowing public gallery. When Thekla appears to give evidence she is booed by crowds outside the court and needs a police escort. After the trial she is held in jail for a few days for her own protection. Under the terms of the witness protection scheme, she disappears from history.

Dr Gaze is found not guilty. His refusal to make out a death certificate for Mabel saves him from prison, although his medical career is ruined. He retires and moves to Mornington.

Travice Tod, who has remained cool throughout the trial, faints when the guilty verdict is announced. He wakens, only to hear the death sentence passed.

Madame Olga has spent most of the time since she was arrested in the prison hospital. She needs to be helped into the dock. Although the death of Mabel Ambrose can be considered her responsibility alone, the public sympathise with her. Within a year, courts in New South Wales will relax the law regarding abortion. Victoria and other states will soon follow. (Australian abortion laws were inherited directly from England. Before 1803, abortion was dealt with in England by ecclesiastical courts and punishment was in the form of penance. In 1803 the *Miscarriage of Women Act*, or Lord Ellenborough's Act, as it was colloquially known, was passed. This made it a capital offence for any person 'unlawfully to administer any noxious and destructive substance or thing with intent to procure the miscarriage of a woman "quick" with child'. An 1861 amendment, the *Offences against the Person Act*, regarded self-administered abortions as a felony.) In consideration of Olga's deafness, a police officer is stationed by her side to relay the verdict to her by shouting in her ear-trumpet. The court is silent as the judge stands.

'I find you guilty under the *Miscarriage of Women Act* . . .'

'He finds you guilty. *Guilty*!'

'And I hereby sentence you to death by hanging . . .'

'It's the death sentence . . . it's the death sentence . . . *the death sentence*!'

When the officer finally gets through to Madame Olga she stands, screams, then collapses. The judge, slightly ruffled, sits and pretends to read a memo on his desk.

Somewhat predictably, Travice Tod lodges an appeal; Madame Olga willingly accepts her fate. Travice's appeal is rejected. A petition is started against the death sentence: Travice receives 3000 signatures and Olga 2000. On March 20 the Executive Council commutes both their sentences – Travice's to six years and Olga's to ten.

Which leaves us with the head. I am disappointed that I have not learned its whereabouts. I am fairly certain that it was not destroyed, as it is exactly the sort of artefact that medical institutions collect for their museums. So it should be somewhere, although as a member of the public I am legally forbidden to photograph it. Institutions have become extremely reluctant to let people into their museums, largely due to pressure on them from an increasingly coy public. And even if I was lucky enough to find the head, I could not tell you where it was, if I ever wanted access to such institutions again. These things, it seems, are no longer of public concern, and are hidden from us.   For our own good.

If I did find the head I could tell them who it belonged to.

THE 5000 FINGERS OF DOCTOR T

I had a cousin two years older than me who played the organ, and whenever we visited her parents' house she would play us Abba songs to a rumba accompaniment. On the way home my mother would tell me that the home organ was a tacky instrument, a degraded piano.

At Easter, my cousin would always receive twice as many Easter eggs as I did. She kept them in a cardboard box. On these visits her mother would tell her to show us her cardboard box, full of the Easter eggs she never ate. My aunt took great pride in this show of her daughter's moral strength. My mother retaliated by sending me to piano lessons.

My mother aspired to the better life, but like most people she had only vague ideas about what was involved. Artists went from door to door selling paintings, and my parents would politely look through folios filled with several copies of each work in different colours. My parents would buy the painting that best matched the decor, or if they liked a painting which used the wrong colours the artist would offer to return with a new, more suitably coloured version within the week.

My father was a building contractor and my mother ran a Copperart franchise. Our house was filled with copper knick-knacks. I met Mr Copperart once when my parents took me to Melbourne on a business trip. Mr Copperart was a big Dutch man who smelled of juniper berries. He took a knick-knack from a shelf in the warehouse and showed me the *Made in England* sticker on the bottom.

He said: 'See that? There's a little town in Taiwan that makes these. Do you know what it's called? *England*.' Then he laughed.

He gave me the knick-knack, a copper sculpture of four monkeys in a row. The first monkey covered his eyes with his hands, the second covered his ears, the third his mouth and the fourth his groin.

My parent's most prized possessions, limited-edition collectables mail-ordered through magazine advertisements from the Franklin Mint, were put in the living room where nobody went because there was no TV. When my parents die, I will inherit these instant heirlooms: a replica BMW in miniature, a painted plate with a picture of an Indian on a horse, a *Star Wars* chess set and a few other things, so that one day I can pass them on to my children.

A velvet painting of a Chinese junk hung on the wall in the recreation room above the piano, a second-hand German-made upright with metal candleholder fittings and dark burns in the wood beneath the fittings where hot candle wax had been left to drip by any number of previous owners. On the other walls were more pictures: a geometric pattern made from nails and string, a studio photograph taken of me when I was a baby sitting naked on a velvet cushion, an abstract design made from copper beaten over a mould and a painting of a tin shed falling to pieces in an outback setting. In one corner of the room stood an exhausted lava lamp. When it was turned on, the decomposed wax would float to the top of the jar and stay there and the water would turn cloudy. We owned three televisions, but I was not supposed to have the television in the recreation room turned on while I was practising the piano.

At first I liked the idea of piano lessons. I liked music and I already owned several records, all of which I had picked for the artwork on the record sleeve. The first record I got was *Ego is not a Dirty Word* by Skyhooks. On the back of the record was reproduced a fictional letter from an obsessed female fan who had cut off her forefinger and sticky-taped it to the bottom of the letter. That severed finger sold me on the record. After that I asked for, and received, a two-record concept album based on H.G. Wells's book *The War of the Worlds,* which came with an eight-page picture booklet; a Leo Sayer greatest hits collection; a record of old novelty hits like 'Monster Mash' and 'My Boomerang Won't Come Back' and something by the Chipmunks. When the piano first arrived I had a lot of fun polishing it and inspecting the machinery inside its wooden case, at least for a couple of hours.

Then one Saturday morning I was sent off to my first lesson with an old woman who lived in a limestone bungalow on the other side of town. On the corner of her Yamaha grand piano was a ceramic bust of Beethoven, which I had seen advertised in editions of the *Australasian Post*. The woman had the offensive odour of an unfamiliar body, intensified by her age and bulk, and I sat next to her on a piano stool with vinyl padding that was stained and indented where dozens of other children, like me, had been forced to sit. She gave me a couple of books on basic music theory, a ruled music book for me to practise drawing notes in, the sheet music to 'When the Saints Go Marching In' and, after a few weeks, when it was beginning to look like I was never going to get the song right, the sheet music to 'Amazing Grace'.

The piano was only the first instrument my mother wanted me to learn. There were more instruments over the following years, and each time I started lessons the teacher would begin by giving me the sheet music to 'When the Saints Go Marching In' and, shortly afterwards, 'Amazing Grace'. You would have thought the songs would have sunk in eventually, but they never did. All I can say is that they made my grandmother happy if I muddled through them for her when she visited. My parents were never particularly pushy: they never entered me in beauty contests or tried to cast me as a child prodigy. I was just no good at saying no to them, at least not directly. I had to discover other ways to do that. Neither of my parents had said that they wanted me to become a pianist; for me to end up as a professional musician was probably the last thing they had in mind. I think my mother wanted me to be a brain surgeon: she had somehow associated playing the piano with

brain surgery, and believed that a person who was good at one was well suited for performing the other. My father, I think, wanted me to become a natural scientist of some sort, an archaeologist or a biologist, going to university and coming out as the new Harry Butler with a beard and a bush hat and my own television show. I failed them both pretty miserably.

The piano lessons continued into the Christmas school holidays. I played 'Amazing Grace' at the end-of-year recital. Obviously, I had not progressed very far. I will tell you a secret, something I would have never told anyone at the time: I never practised. My teacher would tell my mother that she was disappointed in me, and I would cry and tell my mother that I would try harder. But I knew that this was only a temporary solution.

I had started to conduct my own experiments in playing the piano. I spent more time playing in the guts of the piano than I did at the keyboard. I would run my fingers along the strings inside the piano and make sounds like a harp. I would drop things inside the piano, like pencils and books and broken Pez dispensers, and hang paper clips and chewing gum from the strings. I wrote my own 'Music for Piano and Chewing Gum and Pez Dispenser and Pencil and Fake Harp', which sounded a fuck of a lot better to me than 'Amazing Grace' ever would.

This must have been about 1980, post-*Star Wars* but pre-*ET*. I was ten years old. I was born nine months after the first moon landing and you can figure that one out for yourself. My grandmother told me that my parents held a big party for the first moon landing. They bought their first television set for the occasion, and maybe I attach more meaning to this correlation than I should. My parents worked long hours and I spent most of my time alone, so I felt that the television owed me something. I thought that the television should look after me, or at least take on some responsibility for my upbringing, and in many ways it did.

Every Saturday afternoon after my piano lesson I would ride my bicycle to the Sturt Street Cinema in time to see the Monster Movie Matinee. My parents had their own plans for my future. All I wanted to be was the guy who wore the Godzilla suit and got to stomp all over a miniature Tokyo.

My piano teacher started to confront me. 'You are not stupid or slow', she would tell me, 'you just haven't practised, have you?' The way she said it, I thought of all her students I was the only one who hated 'Amazing Grace' and hated practising the piano, and I could hear her implicit threat that there was something wrong with me and I would never amount to anything. Achievement, whether it be in piano lessons or stamp collecting or anything else that was not in the least enjoyable, was character building. If I failed at piano then I would inevitably end up with no job and no friends and no future. This was an important time for my development as a human being, she said, and any shortcomings I exhibited now were sure to be repeated in my adult life.

Every Saturday afternoon I would see a different movie at the Monster Movie Matinee: *Jason and the Argonauts* and *Godzilla versus King Kong* and *Earth versus the Flying Saucers* and *Twenty Thousand Leagues Under the Sea* and *Beneath the Planet of the Apes* and the *Seventh Voyage of Sinbad*.

When I was four years old I watched the *Aunty Jack Show* on television every week. I was afraid not to watch, because at the end of each episode Aunty Jack would say: 'If you don't watch my show next week I'll *rip your bloody arms off.*' If I missed an episode I would sleep in my toybox that night so Aunty Jack could not find me, and I would wake up in the morning with the red outlines of Matchbox cars marked in the flesh of my back where I had slept on them. By the age of ten I had seen *Scream Blacula Scream* and *Deranged* and *The Abominable Doctor Phibes* on television, and more Hammer House of Horror films than I could put a name to and Ken Russell's *Tommy*, with special disturbing memories of Roger Daltrey being put in a syringe-lined iron maiden by Tina Turner, which may be the origin of my fear of needles, but generally I think I turned out all right. What I saw on the television and at the Monster Movie Matinee provided me with a substantial part of my imaginative life. When *Forbidden Planet* played at the Monster Movie Matinee I thought I had discovered a way to escape.

The year is 2257AD. Leslie Nielsen is the commander of United Planets cruiser C-57D, sent to Altair IV to search for survivors of the prospecting ship *Bellerophon* that had landed twenty years before. Nielsen and his team find only two survivors: Doctor Morbius, played by Walter Pidgeon,

and his daughter Altaira (Anne Francis), the rest of the crew having been killed by some unseen monster soon after the *Bellerophon* landed. Morbius lives in a house built above the remains of an ancient and advanced race of beings called the Krell, who became extinct after some sudden and mysterious catastrophe.

During a visit to the underground Krell laboratories, Morbius demonstrates a machine he calls the *plastic educator*, which allows thoughts to be given physical form. Soon afterwards, the members of Leslie Nielsen's crew start being killed off by an invisible monster, in what seems to be a repeat of the *Bellerophon* tragedy. The plastic educator machine has released a monster from Morbius's mind: a *monster from the Id*, a monster from the elementary basis of his subconscious mind, given substance by the Krell machines.

Leslie Nielsen says to Morbius: 'Like you, the Krell forgot one deadly danger: their own subconscious hate and lust for destruction.'

Leslie Nielsen says: 'We are all part-monsters in our subconscious, so we have laws and religion . . . twenty years ago, when your comrades voted to return to Earth, you sent your secret Id out to murder them.'

I went home after the movie and sat there in front of the piano, my wooden educator. Could I help it if my thoughts drifted away from 'Amazing Grace' and the recreation room, across town, and towards that limestone bungalow? Could I stop myself from imagining that strange sucking sound as the great feet sank deep into my piano teacher's front lawn? Could I resist the images that formed in my mind of the front door ripped off its hinges, the body of my piano teacher squashed on the floor like some giant blood-bloated tick, the busted piano stool, the smashed piano and the bust of Beethoven ground into plaster dust?

I was the sole survivor of a once mighty civilisation. Everything had fallen apart over the centuries, until all that was left was the now-demented machinery of life and the vast hoard of plastic replicas the machinery had created. Children were plastic replicas of their parents, little immortality machines, but with each new production run they hoped the latest model would turn out better. They thought their little plastic replicas started out clean, and they would do anything to stop their replicas from getting sullied during their time spent in this dirty world, like they felt they had been dirtied. But maybe the dirt had got in the machinery a long time ago.

I had rid the world of a piano teacher but it made no difference. The world was no better for my efforts. The world would never run out of piano teachers, any more than it would run out of Garfield merchandise or skin replenishing creams or Vegemite Kraft Singles or fake Rolex watches or moronic soft drink commercials or environmentally friendly sanitary pads with wings or faux-marble Formica or self-help books or diet clinics or humorous posters put on the walls of offices that say 'You don't have to be crazy to work here but it helps' or the constant advancements in hair replacement technology or the Three Tenors or Hallmark cards or vinyl cladding or soap operas or Barbara Cartland novels.

Every Saturday morning for the next month I helped my father at a building site, wetting down concrete and stacking bricks, until my mother could find me a new piano teacher. My father's hands were big and looked like fat sausages. They were scarred from years of manual labour, and every morning he put Elastoplast over the cracks in the skin that formed around the joints of his fingers to stop them bleeding too much. He could never play the piano with fingers like that. They were too wide to hit a single key at a time.

  I spent a weekend at the beach with a friend and his family, sleeping in a rented caravan in a caravan park. On the second day I was sitting with my friend on the beach and watching a kid body surfing. After a while the kid stopped moving and just lay face down in the water. My friend said he thought the kid was in trouble. I told him the kid was all right, that he was just faking it. My

friend wanted to get his mother. I told him not to be stupid. We watched the kid as he started turning blue and then my friend started crying so I told him to go get his mother. She came and pulled the kid out of the water and after looking closely at his face she sent us back to the caravan.

I never told my parents what had happened. I never talked to my parents about anything much. They did not read or listen to music. All they did was work and come home late and fall asleep in front of the television and then wake up for long enough to go to bed.

My mother found me a place at the Happy Fingers Institute. My lessons took place on Tuesday afternoons: I had to leave school half an hour early to get to the lesson on time. Every Tuesday I would put my hand up to ask the teacher for permission to leave early, drawing attention to myself like a freak with some horrible medical condition. Then I would get my bike from the bike racks and ride out to the Institute.

The Happy Fingers Institute was run by Doctor

Terwilliker and I was his five hundredth student and his five hundredth set of fingers. We all sat at the same piano, ninety metres long and with two tiers. We all wore our Happy Fingers caps and we all played the same song, the Happy Fingers song, that Doctor Terwilliker had written himself:

> Ten little dancing maidens dancing oh so fine.
> Ten happy little fingers and they're mine all mine.
> They're mine, they're mine,
> Now isn't that just fine.
> Not three, not five,
> Not seven and not nine,
> But ten all dancing straight in line,
> And all of them are mine, mine, mine,
> Yes they are mine, all mine.

Doctor Terwilliker sang the words while we played.

The fence around the Institute was electrified, protecting Doctor Terwilliker from any demons I could summon. Doctor Terwilliker started intruding on my dreams, his hands on mine and his fingers forcing my fingers to play the Happy Fingers song. I was too weak to stop him, and when he finally let me go I would try to hit him but my fists would never quite reach.

Doctor Terwilliker lived alone in a house adjoining the Institute. On the walls of Doctor Terwilliker's living room were framed certificates from correspondence courses and framed letters from pleased parents and watercolour paintings of the English countryside he had painted himself. His furniture was made of wood and there was no television in sight. He said he didn't need one.

Once every three months I would be invited in to his house. He would tell me to sit down and then he would ask how I thought I was going. I would tell him I was going good, then he would hand me a report card which said much the same thing, as well as mentioning that I had great potential, which made my mother happy. She thought I had great potential too.

I was getting older, old enough to know what *cynical* meant. Doctor Terwilliker was a fraud, but no-one else seemed to notice. What did it matter anyway, if none of the parents knew any better and they were happy with what they paid for? Doctor Terwilliker was just as bored as I was, teaching kids the same old songs and praising their ability, or when necessary, their *potential*. Could they hope their kids would grow up to be like Doctor Terwilliker, a lonely old man who refused to own a television?

I could see no end to my bondage. There would always be a Doctor Terwilliker with four hundred and ninety nine other kids to sit at his piano, and every night they would all go home and fall asleep in front of the television and then wake up for long enough go to bed.

In the middle of a lesson I let my fingers go limp and float on the keys like drowned bodies. I looked around at some of the other kids, and now I could see that their fingers were floating too. That day was the last day I touched the piano.

I started turning up to lessons late, and the later I arrived the smaller Doctor Terwilliker seemed to be and the weaker the waving of his baton. My *World Book Encyclopaedia* taught me Zeno's argument against motion: it is impossible to get anywhere because first you must travel half the distance you are going, then half of what remains, then half of what remains, and so on, and you become stuck in an infinite regress from which you can never escape. I was sick of going places, particularly piano lessons. I wanted to get stuck. I wanted to go nowhere. I wanted to drown between the waves.

The next week I was ten minutes late for my half-hour piano lesson. The week after I would be twelve minutes late. I would ride my bike as slowly as I could, until sometimes I was balancing on one spot. Doctor Terwilliker would squint at me as I came in to the room, as if I was starting to disappear from view. I even felt a little sorry for him, but it was too late. I had already begun to get rid of Doctor Terwilliker.

MOCK CHICKEN

I grew up in a town called Mount Gambier in the southeast corner of South Australia. Mount Gambier's main industries were the production of cheese and trees and the subsequent processing of these materials into more useful forms: chipboard and extruded cheddar cheese sticks sealed in transparent plastic tubes. There was also a tourist industry based around the Blue Lake, a large body of water that had collected inside the crater of an extinct volcano. The water from the Blue Lake was particularly blue, but not as blue as the water put in little bottles with labels that read 'genuine Blue Lake water' and then sold to tourists.

My father was a builder, and sometimes he was asked to build fallout shelters under people's houses. The family that lived across the road from us had their own fallout shelter. I was very jealous of their fallout shelter.

The father of the family was in cheese. As I remember, the father was in a position of some authority; I don't think that he was a cheese executive, but he may have been the leader of a small group of cheese workers.

They never ate as well as my family ate. My childhood diet was like an orgy of meat and chocolate and fairy bread and ice-cream sandwiches. After dinner, which we called tea, my parents would drink Irish coffees: instant coffee with a measure of whisky, a scoop of non-dairy whipped cream substitute which came in a tub and would separate into two oleaginous layers on the surface of the hot liquid, and then a sprinkling of cinnamon from a MasterFoods jar. I would prepare myself a similar drink, but made with Milo and without whisky.

Occasionally one of our families would eat tea at the other family's house. If our neighbours came around on a Friday night, which was our fish and chips night, their children would eat all our dim sims. I think they considered dim sims to be too expensive to buy for themselves. To them, eating dim sims at my family's house was an exotic treat.

If we ate at their house, we would invariably be served mock chicken or mock fish or some other processed protein product, along with frozen peas and frozen chips. Perhaps their family had to budget so that they could afford to maintain the fallout shelter. In my family, we had no similar concerns.

Mock chicken could be bought ready-made from the butcher or prepared at home. The main ingredient was sausage mince, to which a packet of chicken noodle soup was added for flavour. This mixture was then shaped into drumsticks. A thick wooden skewer was inserted along the axis of each drumstick, like a surrogate leg bone, then the drumsticks would be coated in breadcrumbs and deep fried. The mock chicken was eaten with the fingers, held by the protruding end of the wooden skewer.

I liked eating mock chicken. At the time I liked mock chicken more than I liked real chicken. The texture was more consistent, and the skewer was much more convenient and less disturbing than real chicken bones. Eating mock chicken was like eating a cartoon chicken.

People no longer make mock chicken, because real chicken has become inexpensive. In the past thirty years, chicken technology has advanced to the point where chicken is one of the cheapest meats available. In the past most chicken meat came from egg-laying flocks. Now special genetic strains of meat broilers have been developed that are rapid growing, disease resistant and have a desirable texture and flavour. A chicken used to take six months to bring to an edible maturity; now the process only takes six weeks. The modern chicken has a high feed conversion ratio: only two kilograms of feed are needed to produce one kilogram of meat. There have also been cosmetic changes made to the birds: meat broilers have white feathers, so that the pin feathers are less noticeable to the consumer, and a lighter skin colour, to make the final product look more appealing. The spread of supermarket chains and the distribution networks designed to service them have also contributed to the easy availability of chicken.

These days I eat a lot of chicken. The chicken is an elegant and highly sophisticated piece of modern technology. In adspeak, chicken has become an affordable luxury: it has maintained an upmarket image while being available for a low cost. The price of food is very important for people on low incomes, and the easy availability of a good meat, like chicken, contributes greatly to their quality of life.　　　　I feel the same way about chicken as I imagine more politically conscious people feel about the democratic system or universal suffrage.

At the same time, I feel a certain nostalgia for mock chicken. Mock chicken was the product of more optimistic times, when people believed that human beings could improve on nature, when the artificial was valued more highly than the real, and before the words *natural* and *artificial* became synonyms for *good* and *evil* respectively.

However, the mock chicken is not the first animal to become extinct as a result of Australian eating habits. The first Australians arrived from the Asian continent around thirty-five thousand years ago. In primary school I was taught that the first Australians were forced here by an approaching Ice Age: as the weather grew colder the people who lived near the Poles began migrating toward the tropics and displacing those who lived there already. Much of the world's water turned into ice, leaving the level of the world's oceans much lower than usual. This made it easy for the first Australians, driven by increased population pressures and food shortages, to come across from the Asian continent in little canoes and rafts. Later, when the Ice Age was over, the water levels returned to their former height and the first Australians were stuck here.

When I think of these first Australians I imagine people much like myself, with similar preferences and tastes. But when the first Australians arrived the landscape was very different. The temperature was on average about eight degrees cooler than it is today. In the southern half of the continent the weather would have been cool to cold, but in the northern half, where the first Australians landed, the weather would have been pleasantly mild.

When I try to imagine how the landscape looked, I picture an endless grassy plain, like a giant paddock, with only the occasional tree and small lake and low hill to break up the monotony. I have to say that this description owes more to my memories of the landscape of cartoons than to anything I have read on the subject of Australia during the Pleistocene epoch.

Inhabiting this landscape I imagine all of the animals that have become extinct since the first Australians arrived:

rhinoceros-sized wombats,

giant koalas,

strange pig-like and tapir-like creatures,

two metre-tall browsing kangaroos,

three metre-tall emus called mihirungs,

huge possums and goannas,

and many other animals whose existence can only be guessed at.

I imagine all of these animals just standing around and eating grass, like prehistoric cows. They have never seen humans before and, with few natural predators, they are quite tame and unafraid of these first Australians. Perhaps they are even curious about their visitors and approach them. At the same time, I imagine the first Australians standing at the edge of this scene, after weeks of sea travel and no fresh food, still holding oars in their hands.

Archaeologists are in disagreement about what

happened when the first Australians arrived. For a long time it was believed that the extinction of most of the large animal species in Australia was caused by climatic changes. A similar explanation was given for the extinctions that occurred when the first New Zealanders arrived in New Zealand, or when the first Americans arrived in America. The first New Zealanders arrived in New Zealand a thousand years ago. The fossil evidence indicates that at least twenty-eight species of large mammals and birds, most notably the giant moa, disappeared between the arrival of the first New Zealanders and the subsequent arrival of Europeans. The first Americans arrived in America eleven thousand years ago. Within a thousand years of their arrival, between seventy and eighty per cent of the continent's large mammal species had disappeared.

In his book *The Rise and Fall of the Third Chimpanzee*, Jared Diamond argues that these extinctions were caused by the arrival of human beings. In the case of New Zealand the evidence is conclusive, given that the event was relatively recent. In America the evidence is convincing although subject to doubt, given that the arrival of the first Americans was around eleven thousand years ago. What happened in Australia, more than thirty five thousand years ago,   is unclear.

Many people imagine the time of the first Australians as a Golden Age, when life was lived in harmony with nature, untouched by the evils of civilisation and industrial society and mass marketing techniques and artificial food flavourings. I also imagine this time as a Golden Age, but my vision of the time is a little different.

Mock Chicken

I am not an archaeologist and, as I mentioned earlier, most of my knowledge of this period of Australian history comes from what I was taught in primary school. But I have one advantage over an archaeologist: I am allowed to say what I would have done in the same situation.

If I were one of the first Australians, standing there with an oar in my hand and surrounded by tame and exotic creatures, my course of action would be clear. I would approach the largest and tastiest-looking creature I could see – probably one of the rhinoceros-sized wombats that I have seen drawn in children's dinosaur books – and hit it on the head. Then I would build a fire and cook the rhinoceros-sized wombat and eat as much of it as I could. Then I would lie down on my back and happily rub my stomach.

The next day I would pick up my oar, walk the short distance south to another tasty-looking animal and repeat the process. At this moment I would know that I had found my calling: for the rest of my foreseeable lifetime, and the lifetime of any children that I might get around to producing, things would be good.

The geoscientist Paul Martin estimated that it took the first Americans a thousand years to travel from the northern edge of the North American continent to the southern tip of the South American continent. He described their progress as a blitzkrieg. Australia is roughly the size of the North American continent; I think it is fair to guess that the Australian Golden Age lasted for half that time, about five hundred years. To travel that distance in five hundred years, the first Australians would have only had to travel eight kilometres south each year. Even I walk further than eight kilometres a year.

Human beings are omnivores: when one food supply dries up they can easily switch to another. There are none of the usual constraints on their numbers as there are for animals with specialised diets. As the first Australians moved south, they left only those animals that were too small or too fast to bother catching, or which reproduced rapidly enough to compensate for the appetites of their hunters. Five hundred years is very little time for a species to evolve a fear of human beings. I imagine that, over time, the first Australians would forget a lot of the hunting and gathering skills that they had arrived with, because they no longer needed them. After a couple of generations, I imagine the first Australians as a race of sedate, overweight, and very content people. Again, this is probably just my fantasy.

The further south they travelled, the colder the weather would have been. Food would have become a little harder to find, and I imagine that the first Australians may have occasionally felt anxious about this, if only once or twice in a lifetime.

I can imagine the ancestors of the first Australians, some five hundred years later, as they approach the southern coast of Australia. I imagine a young man, more restless than his fellow Australians, being the first to arrive at the place where, many thousands of years in the future, Mount Gambier would be built. I imagine this young man to be about the same age as I was when I left Mount Gambier, to provide a convenient reference.

The Blue Lake did not form until ten thousand years ago; when the first of the first Australians arrived it was still an active volcano. Occasionally I imagine the volcano would flare up. When this young man arrives I imagine the skies are dark with ash and smoke and the animals have all left. At least the animals are smart enough to avoid this natural disaster.

For the first time in his life the young man starts to feel hungry. He probably mistakes the hunger pains for the first symptoms of some illness. He hurries south as fast as he can, never imagining that one day this seeming vision of Hell would turn into the kind of place that city people would imagine would be a good place to bring up kids.

Out of breath and in a state of near panic he travels the remaining fifteen kilometres south. About him graze the surviving members of a variety of species:

- a rhinoceros-sized wombat,
- a giant koala,
- a strange pig-like creature and a tapir-like creature,
- a two metre-tall browsing kangaroo,
- a three metre-tall emu called a mihirung,
- a huge possum and a goanna,
- and a few other animals whose existence can only be guessed at.

But for now the young man is not interested in food, at least not directly. He is standing on a beach, staring at a sea which he would have had no reason to expect would be there, and his mind is concentrated solely on the terrible sinking feeling that is growing in his stomach.

THE FINGER GAME

I shall reach great heights, I have been born for a blazing glory. It may take a long time, but I shall have greater glory than Victor Hugo or Napoleon ... There lies within me an immensely powerful glory like a shell about to explode ... This glory will be seen in every one of my works, and will reflect on all the acts of my life. People will research the acts of my childhood and admire the way I played 'Prisoners' base'.

Raymond Roussel wrote two novels, *Impressions of Africa* and *Locus Solus*, several long poems, and two stage plays. After his death an essay, *How I Wrote Certain of My Books*, was published, as he had instructed in his will. In this essay Roussel mentions a trip around the world that he took during the years 1920 and 1921. The trip is only mentioned in passing, and so I will quote the whole passage:

It seems apt that I should mention here a rather curious fact. I have travelled a great deal. Notably in 1920–1921 I travelled around the world by way of India, Australia, New Zealand, the Pacific archipelagi, China, Japan and America ... I already knew the principal countries of Europe, Egypt and all of North Africa, and later I visited Constantinople, Asia Minor and Persia. Now, from all these travels I never took anything for my books. It seems to me that this is worth mentioning, since it clearly shows just how much imagination accounts for everything in my work.

This is not much to base a story on. I do not even know if Roussel came to Melbourne. From the age of twenty, Roussel regularly saw a psychiatrist, Dr Pierre Janet. Janet, who was a Professor of Psychiatric Medicine and a teacher of Jung, published Roussel's case history in a book called *The Psychological Characteristics of Ecstasy*. In Janet's book, Roussel is given the pseudonym Martial, the name of the main character in Roussel's own book, *Locus Solus*. Roussel told Dr Pierre Janet that he was born with a star on his forehead. I also would like to believe that I have a star on my forehead.

Martial, a young neuropath, timid, scrupulous, easily depressed, experienced at the age of nineteen, for five or six months, a mental condition that even he deems extraordinary. Taking up literature, which he preferred to the other pursuits he had followed up to that time, he undertook to write a great work in verse and wished to complete it before the age of twenty. Since this poem was to consist of several thousand verses, he worked assiduously almost without ceasing, day and night, with no feeling of fatigue.

The Finger Game

He felt himself being gradually filled with a strange enthusiasm: '... Everything I wrote was surrounded in rays of light; I would close the curtains for fear the shining rays that were emanating from my pen would escape from the smallest chink; I wanted to throw back the screen and suddenly light up the world. To leave these papers lying about would have sent out rays of light as far as China and the desperate crowd would have flung themselves upon my house. But I did indeed have to take precautions, rays of light were streaming from me and penetrating the walls, the sun was within me and I could do nothing to prevent the incredible glare. Each line was repeated a thousand-fold and I wrote with a thousand flaming pen nibs. No doubt, when the volume appeared, the blinding furnace would be revealed and illuminate the entire universe, but no one would believe that I had once contained it within myself . . .'

Martial Canterel owns 'Locus Solus', a property fifteen minutes from Paris. We are taken around the estate and shown the discoveries and inventions that Martial has made. Raymond Roussel is with us. This place is his invention. We follow a sandy path down a hill to a glass cage ten metres wide and forty metres long. The cage is refrigerated so that the eight corpses inside it do not putrefy. Each corpse is enclosed in a separate cubicle five metres long. Martial takes us past each cubicle and explains what is occurring inside. A plug of *vitalium*, a material invented by Martial, is fitted in a hole above the right ear of each corpse. The vitalium allows the corpses to take on the appearance of life. Each corpse re-enacts a single event, the moment during their lives which imprinted itself most strongly upon their memory. Each cubicle contains a tableau to set the scene for the corpse's actions, and, where necessary, actors assist the corpses in their re-enactments. Every performance is identical down to the smallest detail and is repeated until the plug of vitalium is removed.

1   A dead poet, imprisoned by bandits, disguises a statue of the infant Jesus to look like his infant son. The disguise conceals the fact that his child has escaped with a repentant guard.

2   A man, who died at eighty, reaffirms his wedding vows with his still living wife.

3   A dead actor re-enacts his favourite role in a historical play about Roland de Mandebourg, inventor of the compass.

4   A dead child recites a difficult poem from memory while he sits on his mother's lap. Martial tells us that this opportunity to be with her child again is the only thing keeping the mother from suicide.

5   A dead sculptor crafts small statues of clowns from wax, using tools made from hardened bread.

6   A writer who died of a rare disease relives the painful ray treatment that he underwent to cure his illness. His doctor continues the treatment after his death to see if it has any further effect.

7   A young woman goes insane due to a series of tragic coincidences, and dies soon after. Her husband participates in the performance, gaining relief from seeing her, alive and sane again, for that brief moment before the events of her madness began.

8   A young suicide discovers that his dead father had murdered and then raped his wife, and that an innocent man was jailed for the crime. The young man kills himself by pointing a gun loaded with blanks at his chest and pulling the trigger. The gun is

then reloaded by one of Martial's assistants, so that the man's death can be enacted again.

Roussel would have stayed at the Windsor Hotel in Spring Street. Other hotels, such as the Menzies and Scott's, competed with the Windsor for prestige in the nineteen twenties, but they have all been demolished. I got off the tram at the top of Bourke Street and walked to the front door of the Windsor. I wanted to go inside and ask to see the register. In the register I would find Raymond Roussel's signature, and it would tell me which room he had stayed in. I would then ask if I could see the room.

I got to the entrance and stopped. A doorman stood in front of me. His uniform was the same green as the T-shirt I was wearing. I was too uncomfortable to enter. I imagined the way he would see me, and I felt sure that he would question me if I tried to go in. If I owned the Windsor Hotel, I would not pay some lackey to stand in front of the door. I felt embarrassed and left. I suppose that is what the doorman is there for.

I crossed the road to Parliament House. I was looking for a plaque, like those on Swanston Street that show what the street looked like in the eighteen nineties. After comparing the photograph to the present day, I would average them to arrive at the view during the nineteen twenties. There was no plaque that I could see. I pretended to be interested in Parliament House. Now that I thought about it, I realised my idea was foolish. A lot of people would have stayed in the Windsor from 1920 to 1921. Even if the hotel kept records, I would have had to spend hours looking through them, and if Roussel's signature was there I probably would not recognise it, Finally, if I could not find his name in the records, I would still have to put him in the Windsor. There is no longer anywhere else for him to stay.

The doorman took some guests inside the hotel, and so I crossed the street again and looked in through the glass doors. The interior of the Windsor looked like I thought it would, a set for some period drama. Then I turned around and began to walk to the Princess Theatre.

I started to cross Bourke Street. I could see my tram, the number 96, coming up the hill. There was a large group of people standing at the tram stop, mainly suits going home from work. The dead live on in the faces of strangers, and for a moment I thought that I recognised someone at the tram stop, a friend who had committed suicide several weeks before. I do not know if this happens to other people, but for me, the moment of recognition seems to precede any conscious thought. I felt a little shaken, given the nature of my mission, and I stood at the tram stop and looked at the girl that I thought I had recognised.

I do not know how, or even why, my friend killed herself. I went to the funeral, but I had not met her parents before, and I did not want to intrude on them. Yet I know in detail how Raymond Roussel died because he was a famous man, if only for his family's social position. He also

The Finger Game

left his books. If I was asked to explain why my friend, a girl that I had known for many years, had killed herself on her twenty-fifth birthday, I could not tell you. I do not know what event she would play out in one of Roussel's cubicles.

Next to me, a suit was talking to his mobile phone. 'Hi. I'm at the top of Bourke Street and the tram is coming now. I'll be home in five minutes, not ten. Yeah, that's all.' Instead of catching the tram, I kept walking, past the Imperial Hotel, a bank and a couple of restaurants. As I got closer to the theatre I saw that a bus was parked in front, and the entrance was crowded with pensioners waiting to see *Beauty and the Beast*.

I sat at a table outside the theatre and rolled a cigarette. I smoked and watched the pensioners mill around. Most of them were dressed in brightly coloured tracksuits. A waitress came up to me, so I ordered a cup of coffee. I finished the cigarette and put my hands on my knees. My fingers started to spell out the words that I heard spoken by the pensioners. I do not remember when I invented the rules for the finger game, but I must have been very young. Each digit has a letter assigned to it consecutively, starting with the thumb on my right hand. Once I have reached the letter J, I return to the thumb of my right hand to continue the rest of the alphabet. The fingers of my right hand and both thumbs have three letters assigned to each digit. The fingers of my left hand each have only two letters.

I find myself playing the finger game without realising that I am doing it. I press down on the fingers that correspond to the letters of the words that I hear being spoken, as if I am typing. Sometimes my fingers spell out their own conversations, which go nowhere: yes, of course, I see, don't you? Why not, indeed. The game does not mean anything. It is just a habit that I have no reason to break.

I drank my coffee and left. At this point I had everything I needed to bring Roussel back to life.

Raymond Roussel leaves the Windsor. He tips the doorman just enough for the doorman to be grateful, but not so much that he, Roussel, will appear frivolous. He has left Madame Fredez, his travelling companion, at the hotel. She is little more than a highly paid servant. On another night, Roussel may go to Chinatown to hire a male prostitute, as is his habit, but tonight he is going to the theatre. At Bourke Street a tram has broken down, and Roussel talks to the driver, who is waiting for help to arrive. Roussel is very interested in anything mechanical. In Europe, he sometimes travels in a motorised *roulotte*, or gypsy caravan, which he had built to his own design. The roulotte is equipped with a sitting-room, a bedroom, a study, a bathroom, and a dormitory for the staff of three man-servants. During his travels he has given rides in the roulotte to both the Pope and Mussolini, at their request.

Roussel gives the tram driver some money and continues walking. The Princess Theatre has just been sold, and in 1922 the new owners will commission the architect

Henry White to carry out extensive renovations. Roussel enters the theatre. Roussel's own plays, which were put on at his own expense, were great failures. He has already seen the same play at the Princess Theatre several times. He watches the actors and notes the slight differences in the performance tonight compared to the other nights he has attended. He is interested in the **repetition** of the play more than anything contained within the play itself.

He collects his cloak and tips the cashier. She smiles at Roussel. To the cashier, Roussel is a harmlessly eccentric foreigner. This man, who has come to the theatre so **regularly** to watch the same play, is a subject of amused gossip among the theatre staff. The lead actress thinks that his attention is on her and that the rich foreigner will shortly offer to take her away from this run-down hole.

Roussel returns to his room. Madame Fredez is asleep in her own room. The door that connects their two rooms is sealed on Roussel's side with two strips of white cloth, stuck to the wall with four pads of lacquered wax. Roussel dresses for bed in a white nightshirt, white underpants, black socks and a champagne-coloured vest of fine wool. He takes two tubes of Soneryl, a barbiturate, from a drawer in the bed-side table. He swallows forty tablets, washed down with Fiuggi water. In twelve years, Roussel will die from an overdose of Soneryl in Palermo, Sicily, in a hotel room hardly different from this room. He drags the mattress from the base of the bed and lays it on the floor. Roussel is afraid of falling off the bed. He lies down on the mattress and falls asleep.

Roussel started taking barbiturates to relieve his

neurasthenia, but now he takes them for a different reason. After a long period of sleep, Roussel enters a lucid state of euphoria. On the desk is a silver watch and twelve uncut copies of *Locus Solus*. Light begins to stream from his unconscious body.

From the age of twenty, Roussel has tried to recapture the ecstasy he felt at the age of nineteen while he worked, day and night, on a poem that filled him with a strange enthusiasm. He is now forty-four, and only in a state of drug-induced euphoria can he begin to approximate what he felt at nineteen. In twelve years he will die from his addiction in a Sicilian hotel, while a Fascist demonstration is held on the street outside. Roussel begins to dream, and the two events, his ecstasy and the death that it caused, converge at this third point in time, not in the Windsor Hotel in 1920 or 1921 but right now as I type these words.   We are back at 'Locus Solus', an estate that exists only in one of Roussel's books, but now there is a ninth cubicle.

9   Raymond Roussel, an obscure and largely unsuccessful French author, sits at his desk and writes with a thousand flaming pen nibs while I write with letters made of phosphor. I have taken his place in the role of Martial Canterel, and Raymond Roussel is within me, finally returned to his lost glory.

Moon rock, Smithsonian Institution,
Washington, DC, USA.

SINCE THE ACCIDENT

I was nine years old when *Skylab* fell. Three days before the fall, *Skylab*'s orbit shifted laterally by three degrees. The new orbit took *Skylab* directly over Mount Gambier, the town I lived in. I was sure that I was going to die.

My father was a builder, and sometimes he was asked to build fallout shelters under people's houses or in their backyards. People gave different reasons for why they needed a fallout shelter. In the north of the state was an American base, part of the American early warning defence system, which was sure to be a target for a nuclear attack. And both sides had such an excess of nuclear weapons that someone had probably targeted an innocuous little town like Mount Gambier just for the hell of it.

I saw documentaries on the television about the effects of nuclear radiation and how to properly stock a fallout shelter and what the world would be like after World War Three. I was convinced that the world would end in my lifetime, and probably before I was old enough to have sex.

I would draw up plans of my own ideal house. Above ground would be a small, box-shaped structure built of bricks and with a heavy steel door on one side. Inside the box would be an elevator that would take me down to the sprawling, self-sufficient bunker I would call home.

On July 11, 1979, *Skylab* passed over me, as I waited for the end of the world in the backyard of my parents' house,   passed over North America, the Atlantic Ocean, the southern tip of Africa and finally fell, scattering debris in the Indian Ocean and across thousands of square kilometres of Western Australia.

There is a theory that the Dark Ages began after a meteor crashed in the Yucatan. The collision threw so much dust into the upper atmosphere that the sky went dark, convincing people that the Day of Judgement had arrived. The belief that the end of the world is imminent has been so constant throughout history that I can only conclude the fear has some biological basis. In Charles Darwin's *The Expressions of Emotions in Man and Animals*, he claims emotions serve biological purposes and are subject to the same evolutionary forces that shape claws and teeth. A dog that signals its anger by snarling is more likely to avoid violence and possibly being killed than a dog that bites without warning; snarling, Darwin claimed, arose as a survival trait. Darwin also claimed that emotions persist after they have outlived their original functions, like vestigial or rudimentary organs. A human may snarl when they are angry, but biting is no longer a common form of human aggression.

Perhaps the belief in the threat of imminent human extinction serves some similar biological, if rudimentary, purpose. When I was a teenager they showed *The Day After* at school, but by then I was more impressed with the special effects than any cautionary message that the movie was meant to impart. Now that the Cold War is over, kids are taught about impending environmental holocausts. But I have survived my own Dark Ages. As it turned out, the fall of *Skylab* was the closest Australia ever came to World War Three: a potentially lethal attack by a foreign and, at least symbolically, hostile nation.

When Hal was six, a piece of the falling *Skylab* severed his right arm while he was playing in the sand pit in the backyard of his father's house. Later, his father dug up the fragment. The heat had fused the sand around the lump, which was now encased in glass like a prehistoric insect preserved in amber.

The *San Francisco Examiner* offered a ten thousand dollar reward for the first piece of *Skylab* brought to them. While Hal's father waited at the hospital, Stan Thornton flew to San Francisco with the nine egg-sized pieces of *Skylab* that he had found in his backyard.

Stan Thornton was a seventeen-year-old truck driver who delivered beer to the pubs around Esperance in

Western Australia. A photograph of Thornton appeared on the front page of the *Age* newspaper. He was caught in mid-stride, dressed in a check flannel shirt, flared pants and sneakers, as he changed planes at Tullamarine airport. In one hand he held a sandwich bag, which the newspaper article said contained the pieces of *Skylab*. His face was thin, with a thick jaw, and his mouth was slightly open.

Hal was put in intensive care. Stan Thornton waited in San Francisco for NASA to confirm the origin of **the nine fragments.** Journalists and television crews followed Thornton as he went sightseeing. Stan bought an engagement ring for his girlfriend, Jo Metzel, for eighteen dollars at a discount store. He told reporters that he was going to use the money from the *San Francisco Examiner* to make the initial payment on a house.

Hal's right arm was amputated above the shoulder. The doctor ordered that Hal be kept in the hospital for two weeks, and Hal's father spent the time watching television in the visitors' lounge. The Prime Minister Malcolm Fraser told President Jimmy Carter that we would be happy to return the pieces of *Skylab* if Carter would agree to increase their beef quota. Stan Thornton replied to journalists' questions with one-word answers. The Australian newspapers called Thornton a 'shy hero'. Three men, searching for a man who disappeared near Rawlinna, found a piece of *Skylab* instead and rushed it to Kalgoorlie, their original purpose forgotten. **Police confiscated the fragment,** a two-metre long oxygen tank, when the owner of the property where the oxygen tank had been found decided to claim it for himself.

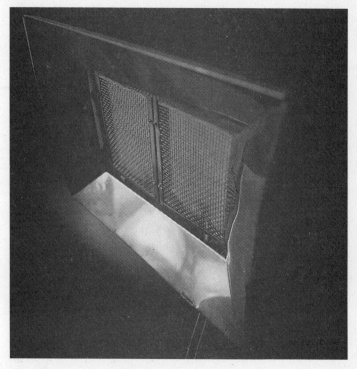

Industrial space heater.

When Hal was brought home from the hospital, his father showed the child the fragment: a twisted metal and ceramic lump the size of a fist. Hal's father placed the fragment on the mantle over the gas heater in the living room. A few months later, it was put in a cupboard. Finally, it was used as a doorstop.

The room was large, part of a warehouse that had been divided up with plywood partitions. A roller door ran most of the length of one wall, and led to an alley littered with Styrofoam, old newspapers, rags and empty beer cans. Next to the roller door was a sink, and a small ceramic urinal. A workbench ran the length of the opposite wall.

Hal sat at one end of the workbench, in front of a desktop computer. A cable ran from the back of the computer to a port on the shoulder of his myoelectric right arm. The computer monitor displayed a wire-frame model of an arm. On the screen, the forearm raised from the elbow and reached forward with an open hand. The arm was fully extended and the hand closed into a fist. Then the procedure reversed, until the arm was hanging down from the shoulder with the fist unclenched, before beginning again. With each repetition, the movement of the arm became smoother and more confident.

A deaf and blind child lay on a rug in the centre of the room. Near the rug, an industrial space heater rested on top of a gas cylinder, the heater element facing the child. The child lay flat on his back. The child's hands picked threads from the rug and then rubbed them on his chest. Discarded threads lay in small piles on either side of the child's torso, indicating that the child had been lying in the same position from some time. The child made clicking noises with his tongue.

A miniature robot walked around the room on six legs made from nitinol wires. The body of the robot was a naked circuit board, with the Radio Shack logo stamped in one corner. A small current, provided by two AAA batteries, was sent through each leg in turn, heating the wire and causing the leg to contract. When the current switched off the wire cooled, returning the leg to its original shape and moving the robot forward a step.

Attached to the front of the robot were two feelers, one at each corner of the rectangular body. When a feeler touched a foreign object, the force of contact would trip a small switch at the base of the feeler. The robot would then turn to avoid the obstacle before continuing forward. If the right feeler was touched, it would turn to the left. If the left feeler was touched it would turn to the right.

Hal unplugged the cable from his myoelectric arm and stood up. Next to Hal a Braun coffee machine, made of black plastic, began to operate after receiving a signal from its internal clock. The coffee machine estimated the temperature and volume of the water in its supply tank, and then set its thermostat according to a set of twenty-five rules burnt into the surface of its microcontroller at a chip fabrication plant in Yokohama.

With his left hand, Hal placed a coffee cup under the nozzle of the coffee machine. He stood there and watched the back-lit liquid crystal display on the front of the machine counting down in one second increments.

The robot, having navigated around an empty cardboard box, began to move toward the centre of the room. The child began to lick his face, his tongue **moving in a circular arc** to the furthest extent of its reach.

Hal flexed his remaining shoulder. The myoelectric arm, controlled by a series of electrodes attached to Hal's chest and stomach, **began to describe a series of trajectories in front of him.** The arm turned at the wrist, elbow and shoulder, but for now the hand remained open.

When *Skylab* was launched the vibrations of lift-off shook free a panel of thermal shielding from the body of the craft. The loose panel severed one of the solar wings that was to have powered the craft when it was in orbit. From then on, the craft was referred to as 'the crippled *Skylab*' in the media, even after most of the damage had been repaired.

Skylab was provided with no motive power of its own. NASA was concerned that the presence of a possibly explosive fuel tank would unnecessarily threaten the lives of the crew members on board the craft. NASA originally believed that *Skylab*'s orbit was high enough for it to remain in space for twelve years. Heavy solar activity decayed *Skylab*'s orbit more rapidly than expected, and it fell after only six years. NASA had planned to use the Space Shuttle to boost *Skylab* into a higher orbit. But because of

Braun coffee machine.

technical and budgetary problems, the Space Shuttle was not ready for flight until several years after *Skylab* had fallen.

The feeler on the right side of the robot touched the child at the right hip. The robot turned left and then continued forward. The same feeler touched the child again, further up the body, and continued, each contact occurring at such regular intervals as to suggest some human agency. When the robot touched the child's stomach the child started to laugh. The child's chest began contracting spasmodically, the head nodded and the lower jaw quivered up and down. The mouth opened with the corners drawn back and the upper lip raised, showing the upper front teeth. The eyebrows lowered, the upper and lower orbicular muscles of the eyes contracted and the **dead eyes opened**. The head of the child became gorged with blood, and the respiration became uneven as the child made a reiterated noise, the inspirations prolonged and continuous and the expirations short and interrupted.

The Braun coffee machine chimed five times when the display reached 00:00. The stream of coffee filling the cup slowed to a dribble and then stopped. Hal stepped back from the coffee machine and stood with his legs slightly apart. The myoelectric arm reached forward, and Hal moved his body to keep the thumb of the arm in line with the handle of the cup. As the hand closed on the cup, a high-pitched whine began to sound from a speaker near the shoulder socket of the myoelectric arm.

The hand lifted the cup from the receptacle in the coffee machine. Hairline fissures appeared on the sides of the cup, and droplets of coffee began to leak down the sides. The whine from the speaker increased in pitch as the pressure exerted by the hand increased.

Hal stepped forward again, and the myoelectric arm put the cup down on the bench, without releasing its hold. He picked up a screwdriver in his left hand and tried to prise the fingers of the myoelectric arm from the cup. Dogs could be heard in the alley outside, barking: the sound from the speaker had passed beyond the range of human hearing.

Hal dropped the screwdriver and turned around. He began to walk rapidly toward the sink on the other side of the room, holding the cup away from his body and to the side. The barking of the dogs grew louder, drowning out the child's laughter, and their forelegs beat against the roller door with a booming noise, like gunshots.

Halfway across the room, Hal stepped on the robot. The body broke in two and the legs splayed out around it like a flattened spider.

The cup shattered, and coffee splashed the face and chest of the deaf–blind child at Hal's feet.

The child began screaming.

The Prisoner's Dilemma: two prisoners accused of committing a crime together are given a set of choices. If one prisoner betrays the other, the betrayer walks out free and the other gets a long sentence. If each prisoner betrays

the other they will both receive a long sentence. If neither accuses the other they both get a short sentence.

The empty shell of a fake security camera was attached, at an odd angle, to the roof in one corner of the shop. A piece of coaxial cable hung down from the back of the camera, the free end having come loose from a socket on the nearest wall. In the corner of the front window was a laminated sign, which claimed that the property was patrolled by a nonexistent security company.

A series of small holes described an arc along the wall behind the shop counter. Each hole contained the flattened head of a conidial bullet. At the back of the shop, behind the counter, was an open door that led to a small office. Inside the office, the shop assistant sat in front of a small television set, watching a pirated videotape of Walt Disney's animated version of Joseph Conrad's *Heart of Darkness*. Above the ceiling of the office was a possum's nest, and the dried residue of possum urine, accumulated over several months, had run down the walls of the office, leaving dark brown streaks on the plastered walls and staining the beige plastic that encased the television set.

Hal entered the shop with his hands in the pockets of his windbreaker. The other customer (Customer 'B') knelt in front of the magazine stand, looking at a row of pornographic magazines. Hal flicked through a rack of old postcards and looked sideways at Customer B. Next to Hal was a faded movie poster showing a young man putting his tongue inside a young woman's mouth. Below the poster was a cardboard display box advertising Hair-In-A-Can.

Electronic componentry.

Hal watched Customer B hide a pornographic magazine between the pages of a folded newspaper. As Customer B straightened up he looked at Hal, and Hal took a postcard from the rack with his left hand and held it in front of his face. On the facing side of the card was a cartoon of a young woman holding up a sign that said 'Student Protest'. The young woman wore a tight mini dress and had large breasts and a distended stomach, as if in the final months of pregnancy. A middle-aged man with the red face of an alcoholic stared at her with his mouth open and bulging eyes. The caption read: 'Blimey Love, I don't think you protested enough!'

Customer B crossed the counter and placed the correct change for the price of the newspaper on the Formica-covered surface. Customer B nodded to the shop assistant. Then the shop assistant grunted.

When Customer B had left the shop, Hal approached the counter himself and took one of several foil-wrapped chocolate eggs from an orange and white display box. He placed the egg on the counter and unwrapped the foil, using the thumb and fingers of his left hand. Next, he separated the two moulded halves of the chocolate egg by digging his thumbnail into the dividing seam.

Inside the egg was a hollow plastic cylinder of a light blue colour, moulded from two separate pieces held together by a joggled joint. Hal put one half of the chocolate egg in his mouth. Then he picked up the capsule and squeezed it between the ball of his thumb and the knuckle of his forefinger until the two ends of the capsule came apart.

Hal placed the two pieces of the capsule on the counter. Inside the capsule, like the dismembered victim of serial killer, were the disassembled pieces of a pink plastic boy. The limbs and the head of the boy were designed to be attached to the torso with ball and socket joints, allowing the boy to adopt different poses, as well as to be neatly packed into the small volume of the plastic capsule.

Hal put his left hand back into his jacket pocket. the head and one arm of the plastic boy fell out of the capsule and lay on the counter.

The shop assistant turned to look at Hal, and then turned back to the television set. The video was almost over. Mickey Mouse, dressed in his Steamboat Willie outfit, had just rescued Kurtz from the natives. As the pair ran toward the steamboat, the natives began firing arrows. Mickey pulled Kurtz over the bow of the steamboat just as the first volley of arrows reached them. The arrows embedded themselves in the hull, pinning Kurtz's shadow to the side of the steamboat. Mickey yanked hard on Kurtz's arm, and Kurtz's body separated from his shadow with a tearing sound. Kurtz screamed, and the shadow went limp.

Mickey left the unconscious Kurtz safely hidden behind a bulkhead, and then crawled into the cabin of the steamboat. Mickey reached up and pulled the cable attached to the steam whistle on the roof of the cabin.

The whistle made a sound like an air raid siren. The natives stopped firing and threw themselves on the ground, their arms over their heads, like schoolchildren during a nuclear attack drill. The steamboat pulled away from the shore, leaving the natives lying on the ground in a 'duck and cover' position, waiting for the flash of light and the ground-shaking explosion.

When the shop assistant heard the postcard rack hit the ground, he stood up with the remote control in one hand. On the screen, Kurtz woke up and looked at the departing shore, then looked at Mickey Mouse and said: 'The horror. The horror!'

Mickey said: 'Don't worry, Mister Kurtz, you're safe now.'

The shop assistant paused the video on a close-up of Mickey's face, and then walked into the empty shop. The postcard rack lay on the floor. The egg and its contents lay on the counter.

The shop assistant stuck his head out of the door of the shop, and watched Hal running down the street and around the nearest corner. Then the shop assistant kicked the postcard rack into a corner and returned to the office.

The right side pocket of Hal's windbreaker was ripped open along the front seam, and Hal held the detached prosthesis under the pit of his left arm like a rolled up newspaper. Between the fingers of the myoelectric arm were several crumpled postcards. Hal kept running.

No matter where Hal runs, at each major intersection that he passes are a pair of competing service stations and a

Remote control.

McDonald's restaurant, and on the remaining corner is either a KFC or a Hungry Jack's franchise. Between these junctions are a variety of stores:

a Mr Muffler,
an Amcal Chemist,
a Coles supermarket,
a Liquor Barn,
a Blockbuster Video,

like the basic building blocks of some vast and stable molecule. Hidden among the franchises are the tiny, family-run businesses, milk bars, fish and chip shops, hamburger shops, and take-away chicken shops with names like

the Chicken Haven or
the Chicken Barn or
Chicken-A-Go-Go or
Chick 'N' Drive or
the Chicken Hide-Out or
the Hungry Chicken or
the Chicken Bar or
the Chicken Coterie or
Chickadees Takeaway or
the Golden Chicken or
the Chicken Corner or
the Chicken Deli or
Chicken Plus or
the Chook Stop or
the Chicken House or
Chicken Town or
Chicken Village or
Chicken World or

the Chicken Cellar or
Dial-A-Chicken or
the Cheeky Chook or
Charcoal Chicken Supreme or
the Chicken Diner or
the Gourmet Chicken or
the Chicken Gourmet or
Chicken Munchies or
the Chicken Inn or
the Chicken Shoppe or
Chicken Bites or
BBQ Chicken or
Big Bird Chickens or
Chicken Little's or
Kenny Khicken or
Chicken Carnival or
Chicken Chompers or
Cheep-A-Chicken or
the Chicken King or
Celebrity Chicken or
Chubby's Chicken or
Chicken Delights or the
Golden Rooster or
Luv-A-Chicken or
La Chicken or the
Tasty Chicken or
the Chicken Spot or
the Chicken Pig Out Pad or
Chicken Nibbles or
Rooster on the Run or

> the Rooster Ranch or
> the Hitching Rail or
> Roosters Choice or
> the 'R' 'U' Hungry Chicken Pagoda or
> Chicken Feed or
> Yummy Chicken or the
> Chicken Factory.

Each shop has its own menu and its own mascot: a cartoon chicken, living or dead, its painted body scratched and flaking at the edges, and each owner dreams of having a franchise at every major intersection. And far above, the spy satellites maintain their geostationary orbits and send continuous streams of images back to earth.

For Hal's twenty-first birthday, his father gave him a videotape of the 1979 Miss Universe pageant. The 1979 pageant was held in Perth, as part of Western Australia's 150th anniversary celebrations. The organisers called it 'a celebration of peace, friendship and justice broadcast live by satellite to seven hundred million viewers in forty-eight countries'. Miss Nicaragua, Patricia Chamarro, retired from the event after her family received death threats from Nicaraguan rebels. Miss China retired after claiming that the contest had an 'anti-Asian' bias. *Skylab* fell the day after the opening ceremony, two weeks before the final pageant.

In the days leading up to the pageant, the contestants posed for photographs with people who had found *Skylab* **debris,** kissing the men coyly on the cheek, and appeared on television wearing bright blue T-shirts computer-printed with pictures of *Skylab*.

There was an audience of seven thousand people and eight television cameras at the Perth Entertainment Centre. At one side of the stage was the oxygen tank from *Skylab*, provided for the ceremony by the Kalgoorlie police. A team sent by NASA to supervise the collection of *Skylab* debris inspected the tank on the stage while the contestants rehearsed. Robert Grey, head of the NASA team, said: 'Can't we move that piece of junk away so we can watch the girls?'

Dick Clark hosted the show with Donny Osmond, and the two men sang duets while the contestants were off-stage changing outfits. Prerecorded segments showed the contestants enjoying themselves in the outback and relaxing by the swimming pool at their hotel. After each commercial break, a deep-voiced American announcer described the history and tourist sites of Western Australia in sixty-second segments. At the end of the night Miss Venezuela, Marita Salayero, was announced as the winner.

The outgoing Miss Universe, Margaret Gardiner of South Africa, placed the Miss Universe sash around Miss Venezuela's waist, and then placed the crown upon Miss Venezuela's head. She stood facing the new Miss Universe and to the left. She cupped her right hand under Miss Venezuela's chin, the fingers held straight against Miss

Venezuela's left cheek and the thumb almost touching her lower lip. Then she kissed Miss Venezuela on the right cheek, and held the pose until the photographers had taken all the photographs they wanted.

More than thirty contestants, journalists and photographers crowded around the new Miss Universe, and the plywood platform they were standing on collapsed. The oxygen tank from *Skylab* rolled into this new depression, crushing Miss Turkey, Fusun Demirtan, and breaking the right leg of Dian Bartolo, the current Miss Malta. Miss Brazil, Meartha Dacosta, had her dress ripped from her body. Miss England, Carolyn Seward, winner of the Miss Photogenic Award, received minor injuries. Miss Japan, Yurika Kuroda, judged the most friendly entrant and recipient of the Miss Unity award, was treated for shock. Miss Bermuda, Gina Saison, who came in second place and won Miss Congeniality, received minor cuts and bruises. Miss Australia, Kerrie Dunderdale, was unharmed and unplaced.

In the newspapers from the next day, photographs of the accident ran side-by-side with the photographs of the crowning. The expressions on the faces of the injured girls are indistinguishable from the expression borne by Miss Venezuela while receiving her award. Only the captions beneath each image distinguish which photographs were taken before and which after the accident.

Transformer.

Hal's father owned a chicken abattoir, Chicken Little's Chicken Factory. The chickens arrived at night in plastic cages, fifteen to a cage, except in summer when the chickens were in danger of suffocating if more than ten chickens were packed in each cage. The chickens have to be packed in tightly: otherwise they would panic during the trip and peck and claw each other to death. Chickens like the company of other chickens.

Immigrant women take the chickens and shackle them by their legs to a moving overhead conveyor belt. The remainder of the process is **automated**. First the chickens are stunned with a forty-volt charge. The heads of the insensible chickens are **held in position by a guide** while a rotary blade slits each chicken's throat. The conveyor takes the chickens over a trough, where the bodies are allowed to bleed for ninety seconds. The blood is collected, dried, and used for stock feed. The bodies pass through a scalding bath to loosen the feathers and remove the skin's epidermal layer; then they pass through a large machine, like something designed by Doctor Seuss, filled with gyrating rubber fingers which rub off the chicken's feathers. The feathers are collected and used in stock feed. A series of water jets wash the bodies, first from the top and then from the sides. A V-shaped blade catches each chicken around the throat and severs the head, which then falls into a collection bin. An overhead drill cuts a hole through the anus of each chicken, loosening the mesentery tissue, a hook ties the anus, a suction device pulls the anus to the outside of the bird and a blade cuts it off. A scoop removes the guts through the anal cavity, as well as any eggs still in the chicken's body. The eggs are used as industrial egg ingredients in cake mixes, custards and mayonnaise; the giblets are sold separately. The outside of the body is sprayed down to remove any internal organ residue, the neck hole is drilled from below and then spray cleaned. The neck bone is broken, and a vacuum nozzle pushes through the neck and sucks clean the inside of the bird. A final spray cleans the bodies both inside and outside, and then a blade severs the bird's feet. The bodies fall into a chilling bath, while the conveyor, still holding the feet, continues a short way and then releases the feet into a collection bin. The feet are used in pet food. A water screw, one of Leonardo da Vinci's many inventions, **pushes the bodies through the chilling bath;** then they are dried, sorted and vacuum-packed in a PVC barrier bag.

In a small room of the warehouse, defined by plywood partitions, was a camp bed, a desk and a chest of drawers. The myoelectric arm lay on the desk, plugged into a wall socket, recharging its batteries. On the floor next to the bed was a bakelite ashtray from Hawaii and a hardcover edition of Charles Darwin's *The Expression of Emotions in Man and Animals*, with a dark blue fabric cover and a spine covered with Gaffa tape.

The body is found hanging from the conveyor belt by the right arm. The left arm is missing, the result of a previous accident. The current, a charge of forty volts, is considered insufficient to electrocute a human being. The security camera, either by accident or on purpose, had been turned off. No further details of the accident are known.

Hal, like the proverbial chicken, crosses the road. A passer-by yells:
 'Look out. The bus!'
 Hal looks up, and both arms raise themselves over his head to protect him from the impact.

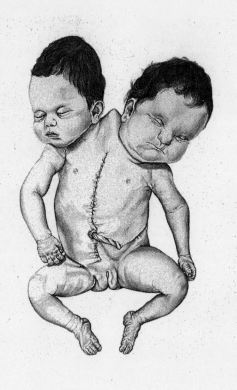

TERATOLOGY

The reason I am aggressive is that I have a smaller penis than my brother. This is not surprising, since even a single person is **not symmetrical**. A single person has one foot larger than the other, one hand is larger, both sides of the face are subtly different, and so on. Perhaps the reason my penis is smaller is because of my diet. We have separate stomachs and **rather different tastes**. Maybe if I suggested this theory to a researcher, maybe a nice, young researcher, she might take up the offer. She could take daily measurements of my penis – by hand of course. That would be much better than doing it yourself.

Masturbation is something we learnt early. It was, I think, the **discrepancy** that first brought us to masturbate. This is the way it happened. We were standing in front of a mirror and my brother pointed at my penis. He made some comment about the size of it, some childish comment. I had, I must admit, noticed this **discrepancy** before. So I played a trick on him. I told him that he was pointing at his penis, not mine. It is like this, I said. A person's left brain controls the right eye, the right arm, the right leg, and in our case, the right penis. So the right-hand penis is yours. He looked at me, and then he put his fist around it. To maintain the symmetry, I grabbed his. I must say that, given our configuration, this is probably a more comfortable way to go about it.

Another thing about my brother: he snores. I read in a newspaper that a way to stop snoring is to lie on your side. Obviously that is not an option available to us.

I told that story to a researcher once, and she laughed. She was a nice woman, who was always friendly to me. **I liked her a lot.** She must have known how I felt about her, because one day when I asked her if she had a sister she screwed up her face and left the room. Soon afterwards she was moved to another ward. This, I thought at the time, is the problem with our society today. There are no more arranged marriages. In the old days we would have been married by now. Chang and Eng married two English girls who were sisters. The Tocci brothers, Giovanni and Giacomo, married sisters too. When the Tocci brothers were born their parents looked upon them as a godsend. This was because they were poor.

I would **really like to meet** a pair of identical twins. Much research goes on with identical twins. If one twin has cancer, for example, and the other doesn't, a lot can be learned by doing **comparison tests** on them. **I like to imagine** that somewhere in this building they conduct research on identical twins, and one day when my brother and I are taking a walk we will meet two beautiful twins, **fall in love,** and so on. I have never asked anyone if that sort of research is conducted here. My reputation is

Teratology

bad enough as it is. Still, I do not want to spend the rest of my life lying in bed and jerking off my brother whenever he gets the urge.

He is insatiable. At least I think he is the one who is insatiable. It is hard to tell, since I often have to anticipate his desires. If a nurse bends over too far while she attends to us and we catch a glimpse of her cleavage, a session of masturbation is inevitable. Sometimes I wonder if he knows the truth. I am not going to tell him. To be honest, I do not talk to him very often. We really have very little in common.

I like to think that the nurses reveal themselves to us on purpose. The nurses tend to be more earthy than the researchers. The researchers are usually distant and cold, but I respect that. Their training makes them look at things objectively. I have noticed that the nurses like my brother better. They have probably heard about the discrepancy.

We are not bad looking. Women should find us attractive. To start with, there is the novelty of the situation. I have read that many people have sexual fantasies about encounters with people like us. Chang and Eng had two families. They would alternate spending three days at each house. Chang had ten children, and Eng had twelve. I think that says something. Rosa and Josepha Blazek, the 'Bohemian twins' as they were called, were very active sexually. Rosa gave birth to a son at the age of thirty-two (this was in 1910). Her parents would not allow her to marry the father of the child. If they had married, the child's father would have legally been a bigamist. Of course, in those days this was all a matter for the church. Saint Hilaire decided that, since the rite of baptism is performed on the head of each recipient, the number of heads decides the number of souls. Yet in a case recorded by Ambroise Paré in 1546, of a monster having two heads, two arms and four legs, he found only one heart, and concluded it was one infant. I do not agree with either of them. If the purpose of the human race is to reproduce, then the solution to this problem must lie in a tally of the generative equipment.

Paré also wrote that the cause of monsters was either **too little or too great** a quantity of seed. Too little and the infant would be lacking parts, too much and the infant would have too many. I wonder what my father would think of that.

I wonder what sort of monster would be born from all the sperm wasted on our hospital sheets.

Our daily routine goes something like this: I wake up in the morning and I write for a while. About nine months ago I bought a laptop computer, which is the perfect size for writing in bed. I put a password on it so that my brother cannot read what I write. The password is my brother's name, which is a little joke for my own amusement. Someone trying to get into a computer is not going to guess that the password is their own name. When he wakes up I usually make him wait until I have finished writing. The laptop has an older-style LCD screen that cannot be seen from an angle, so he just sits there while I type, or he watches the television. Then we have a shower and drink some coffee. **I like to have a cigarette in the morning,** but my brother always complains. He is worried that he will catch cancer from me. He smokes too, when people come to visit, but he calls himself a social smoker, so it doesn't count. He threatened that if I do not stop smoking he will take out a court order against me. I told him that he watches too much television. That sort of thing only happens in America anyway.

Then the researchers come. They check our blood pressure and ask us how we slept. Sometimes they take blood or urine samples, or anything else they can get a hold of. They ask for sperm sometimes but I always refuse. I tell the researchers that I would be too embarrassed.

We get plenty of attention from the staff. We have our own occupational therapist to deal with all our aches and pains. There is something about the designation occupational therapist that seems inappropriate. It seems to imply that, if the therapy is occupational, then the disability should be entered as the person's job description. After the therapy they conduct psychological tests, which I either go along with or I don't, depending on the weather, among other things. I like to be difficult.

Then we are free to do what we want, if no further tests have been scheduled. We might go for a walk to the hospital bookshop to see if any of the books I have ordered are in. I exhausted the hospital library a long time ago. My brother likes us to walk through the gardens so that he can talk to the other patients. I avoid participating in these awkward conversations. The other patients remind me of domesticated animals. I do not understand why my brother enjoys talking to them.	When I think about it, I realise the real difference between us is that he has accepted his captivity and I have not. I cannot respect him for giving in.

The only time our routine is broken is when a television reporter comes to do a story on us. When we were younger, television crews would come from all over the world on a weekly basis. These days they come less often, perhaps because we are not as cute now as when we were younger. The last interview we did was with Ray Martin for *Sixty Minutes*, a follow-up to a story they made a few years ago. I had thought that Ray Martin was a smarmy git from seeing him on television, and meeting him confirmed it. He asked us all of the usual questions, which were either patronising or leading or both, and my brother replied with the usual answers. During the interview I began to feel very angry with this man. Finally, to close the interview, he told us that we were very brave individuals. I said to him, what does that mean? What are you talking about? Nothing has happened to us. This isn't Kafka's *Metamorphosis*, we didn't wake up one morning and discover we had turned into monstrous vermin. We were born like this. We aren't brave. If anything, we're an anachronism. If our mother had been given an ultrasound like everyone else, we would have been aborted. We're fucking freaks.

Sixty Minutes decided to edit that bit out. I think the literary reference threw them.

My ambition is to become a writer of fiction. It may not be a very practical choice, but I have little need to be practical. That does not mean that I cannot justify my ambition: I can provide a concrete rationale. First, writing is the only activity that I can do without needing to include

my brother. Second, it enables me to maintain a degree of anonymity. I have been published in several magazines (under a pseudonym), and everything considered, I am reasonably successful. There are also other, less tangible benefits to being a writer. Since nobody reads any more, writing is a dead profession: an anachronism. So the writer does not have to participate in the real world the way that other types of artists do. The role is very passive. I can be defined solely in terms of words on the page. As far as the reader is concerned, I do not even need to exist.

My brother also likes to write. Today I found a letter written by him on the bedside table. The letter is not addressed to anyone, but it was obviously left out for me to find. In places the ink is smudged, as if by tears:

He has been condescending towards me since we were little. I don't know where I stand with him. Every time I am on the defensive because I never know how hes going to be whether hes going to be patronising or just damn nasty and on about 3 occasions actually nice (although in a very superior tone) and when hes nice Im grateful, which is totally fucked because up until 2 days ago Id never done anything to him for him to treat me like that. Im not the only one whos felt his hostility though Cas & Bindi both originally found his attitude towards them the same as I do. Cas to the extent where she hated him wanted to punch him & just wanted to stay away, for some reason he has laid off them now but not me.

He takes his lead from the doctors who are also patronising towards me more often than not and because he has such a full on personality he feels quite safe in following suit in fact being more arrogant, I cant ward him off because he is a more full on person than myself and also bigger so I cant do anything about his victimisation except boil but he makes up for it by listening to me ie when I told him about the rope & even tho 8 times out of 10 he does take out things that he is frustrated with out on me it sort of balances out.

With him it doesnt balance he is quite cocky because he has them behind him with no redeeming or caring or occasionally sensing you need a hug & giving you one, or coming out with interesting conversation qualities.

But I wish they could see it from my point of view – theyve waltzed into our happy life & turned it upside down, I used to love living here its an ordeal almost now the consolation would have been having Cas & Bindi climb into bed with us & talking to them all night except he fucking chased them away. I wish theyd come back.

For every 1 good thing about him there are about 5 really bad things that totally overshadow it eg. theres this constant stream of visitors & couch tourists that eat all the food I never get any of it. I just dont eat any more apart from bread & cheese & milk & coffee if theres any left. ½ of them you cant trust Im constantly on the visitor vigil because Ive got a bass an amp and a sewing machine & I dont want them to go the same way as the change Ive left on the table & my cigarette stashes in the bedroom, I know I should hide things but Ive always considered other peoples rooms & possessions tabu but it seems I am alone in this sentiment because these guests are part & parcel of it. There is no room for my friends to come over & when they do they just find the place as it is now unbearable ie Lisa left today after 1 cuppa because she couldnt handle the fighting, Robbie used to come around and drink & talk & smoke but he doesnt like it here anymore. I cant blame him.

I would defend myself from my brother's attacks, but the reader is not obliged to believe me. I try to write the truth, but there is no way for me to judge my reliability as a narrator. I could describe my feelings towards my brother and analyse my motives, but I would lack my brother's candour. It seems that stupid people have a monopoly on sincerity. Instead, like Sterne, I will tell you about his hobby-horse. My brother collects Barbie dolls. He started when he found a Barbie doll left by a discharged patient. Now he has hundreds of them. Most of his free time is spent dressing up his dolls and corresponding with other collectors. He bids by phone at auctions held around the world for particularly rare Barbies, which can cost thousands of dollars.

    He has several of the original 1959 Barbies with the hard Germanic face and sideways glance,

> a 'Red Flair' Barbie in a Balenciaga coat,
> Barbie 'Golden Evening' with bubble-cut hairdo and bellskirt evening dress,
> 'Sweater Girl' Barbie,
> 'Winter Holiday' Barbie in a nouvelle vague outfit and white lipstick,
> 'Plantation' Barbie,
> 'Graduation' Barbie,
> a 1963 'Student Teacher' Barbie with pointer and globe,
> 'American Airlines Stewardess' Barbie and
> a 'Barbie Goes to College' set with a drive-in, dorm and malt shop.

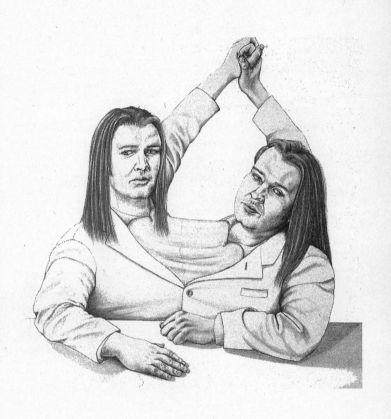

There is 'Ken à Go-Go' with a flowered guitar, Beatles wig, striped shirt, and stovepipe pants,
a 'Suede Scene' Ken with 'Gu-ruvy Formal' Nehru outfit and
a 'Now-Look Ken Doll' with Neil Diamond pouf.
My brother has the Barbie campervan,
a Barbie 'Little Theatre' for her to dance 'The Nutcracker Suite',
a 'Barbie Loves McDonald's' playshop with a blue McDonald's clerk uniform for Barbie to wear
and a 'Barbie's "Wedding Day" Set' with a 'Wedding Party' doll case that stands in the centre of my bookshelf, under protest.

Then there are his favourites, the factory seconds once sold cheap to employees, until Mattel discovered these mutant Barbies were being resold to collectors, and began destroying them instead. He keeps them hidden from me: microcephalic Barbies with foreshortened heads, or twisted arms and legs, with blotched skin or cheeks sprouting stray clumps of hair like warts. Sick dolls, the vinyl flesh bubbled with syphilitic chancres, twisted fingers and hair and eyes emerging like malignant teratomas from their guts. Do you understand now? And two days ago his latest acquisition came and he showed it to me: two Barbies, side by side and joined by a lump of vinyl from chest to hips, naked in a transparent display case. So I grabbed it and threw it out of the window, and then I took Cas and Bindie and, dragging him screaming, into the kitchen I put Cas and Bindie head first into the In-Sink-Erator and ground them into vinyl shavings. The sad thing is, both Cas and Bindie were part of his collection. They were his favourites. His friend Lisa is a Miss Barbie and Robbie is a fucking GI Joe. You thought they were real people?

The truly sad thing is that I am stuck with him for the rest of my life and when we die we will be interred in a great big specimen box filled with formalin and they will put us on display. And visitors will come along, and point at us and say: My, that one had a small penis.

STUCCO

In the center of the field was a gigantic pile of sets, flats and props. While he watched, a ten-ton truck added another load to it. This was the final dumping ground. He thought of Janvier's 'Sargasso Sea.' Just as that imaginary body of water was a history of civilization in the form of a marine junkyard, the studio lot was one in the form of a dream dump. A Sargasso of the imagination!

        Nathanael West, *The Day of the Locust*

It takes a long time for him to settle down in the coffin. There is no light and the ground is cold beneath him. But eventually he stops fidgeting, and a bit later he stops worrying. He pulls the blanket up over his legs. Maybe this was how his grandfather had felt, or at least he would have felt if he had not chosen to be cremated. Death is a lot more pleasant than Stucco had expected.

  Death is like a day off school. When he was a kid he took a lot of sick days, almost always with fake illnesses. His mother would set him up on the couch in the lounge-room, with the curtains drawn and a blanket and pillows and the television on. There had been only two television channels when he grew up, the government channel and a commercial channel, but until the afternoon the government channel broadcast a test pattern and the commercial channel broadcast chat shows and American soap operas. So he always watched the test pattern.

The test pattern looked to him like a friendly, Mondrian-inspired face. He liked the test pattern, and he liked the music that played while it was on: instrumentals like 'Spanish Flea' and the 'One-Note Samba', and themes from television shows and movies, like the theme from *Doctor Who* and from *Zorba the Greek*, and the theme from *The Third Man* and Hugo Montenegro's version of the theme from *The Good, the Bad and the Ugly*. And when the theme from *The Good, the Bad and the Ugly* played he would get off the couch, his imaginary illness forgotten, and trot around in circles, slapping himself on the rump like a cowboy riding an imaginary horse.

He has planned his revenge. He knows the face of the man who will open the coffin as well as he knows his own. When the lid opens, he will sit up and take the man's nose between his teeth and bite as hard as he can. As his mouth fills with blood, he will say: 'Who's laughing now?'

He sticks his thumb in his mouth, to simulate the situation.

He says: 'Who's waughing now?'

He hears the distant sound of a train approaching.

Stucco

His official title is The Man With No Name, but nobody calls him that. They used to call him Stranger, or Gringo, or, sometimes, Blondie. Then, during a barroom brawl, an inexperienced extra fired off a revolver next to his head and the jet of exhaust gasses blew off his nose and left him deaf in one ear. Doc made him a new nose out of tin, but it gave him a rash. Doc got it right the second time, with a nose made from plaster of Paris. Now everybody calls him Stucco.

The loss of his nose ruined his career. They tried soft-focus on the close-ups, but the audience could still tell. Losing an eye would have been no problem. A glass eye is a reasonable substitute. He squints anyway, and the brim of his hat casts a dark shadow over his face, level with his cheeks, in the harsh sunlight. He can still do profiles with the sun behind him and his face in silhouette. But a man without a nose is hardly a man at all, as far as the box-office is concerned.

Since he lost his nose people treat him differently. Instead of peeking at him through shuttered windows, they stand in plain view and watch him. Some of them laugh. The grave-diggers spit at his feet. He can still shoot, but the people have lost their fear of him.

Now he is stranded in a B-grade town and can go no further. The town used to be called Redemption, then Hope, then Hell, but for now it is Untitled.

At night everybody sleeps in a trailer park hidden from sight behind a nearby hill. Some nights he sits on the roof of his caravan and looks up at the unpainted black velvet sky and plays Charles Bronson's theme tune from *Once Upon a Time in the West* on the harmonica he keeps tied on a cord around his neck, overblowing the final note so that the pitch, as it bends, clashes dissonantly with the reverb channel on the soundtrack. The stars wink, and sometimes a bulb blows, and if the bills have not been paid, there are no stars at all.

He rides into town on a mule. He is called Stucco, although that is not his real name. His real name is The Man With No Name, or The Man. Everybody calls him Stucco because he wears a prosthetic nose made of plaster. His nose was shot off by an inexperienced stunter who fired off a pistol too close to Stucco's face. The accident also left Stucco partially deaf – he used to be soft spoken, but now he speaks too loudly and too often.

He wears a plaster nose because he is too cheap to buy a tin nose. Tin is expensive, but stucco is cheap. The whole town is built of stucco. Stucco will never run out.

He rides down the centre of the main street. On either side, the townspeople laugh as he rides past. The townspeople are all stock characters:

the grizzled prospector;
the evil cattle baron;
the callous youth who dreams of being a gunfighter;
Doc;

>   the ineffectual and corrupt sheriff;
>
>   the Chink grave-digger;
>
>   the tavern-owner;
>
>   the hard-working farmer with his blonde wife and his precocious son;
>
>   and Gloria, the whore with the heart of gold.

The town has no name, because nobody has thought one up for it. The name of the town should relate to the action that takes place in it. For now, no action has been decided upon.

This town is Stucco's last chance. He has ended up here because he has nowhere else to go. To leave, he has to prove himself to the producers and the box-office. Somehow, he has to make some meaning out of this situation to redeem himself.

When Stucco lost his nose he lost his confidence and his sense of direction. The grizzled prospector told him that the Japanese believe the self is located at the tip of the nose. Stucco asked the prospector what he should do. The prospector told him to use a lot of dialogue, because dialogue is easy to write and cheap to film. Stucco said he would consider his advice.

The prospector also said: Techniscope is cheaper than Cinemascope. Nobody ever walked out of a film because the boom swung into shot. Dub in the dialogue later. Keep the dialogue stylised and laconic. Be terse. There are only three basic plots – which one are you going to pick?

Revenge, Stucco said. No. I don't know. Revenge will have to do.

Stucco rides into town on his mule. He hitches the mule outside of the town's only saloon. He slings the saddle bag over his shoulder and then walks through the swinging doors into the saloon. The grizzled prospector is standing at the bar, talking to the saloon owner. The evil cattle baron sits at a table, playing cards with his hired guns.

Stucco tips back his hat. He lights a match on the sole of his boot and then lights his cheroot. He rubs the stubble on his chin between the fingers and thumb of his left hand. He squints and looks around the room. Gloria, the whore with the heart of gold, stands leaning against the balcony at the top of the stairs. She turns away when he catches her eye.

Stucco opens his mouth a little and then shuts it again.

A high organ note plays.

Stucco tries to imagine his audience, to better understand what they want to happen next. He is only successful in remembering his weekend visits to his grandfather when he was a child. By that time his grandfather never left the house, and spent the days propped up on the couch in his living-room, watching westerns on the television. Stucco remembers that the curtains were always drawn and the room was always dark. Stucco remembers the rug drawn across his grandfather's legs and the stubble on his grandfather's face. Stucco remembers the magazine rack full of Louis L'Amour novels next to the couch and next to the magazine rack, a side table with an ashtray, a packet of cigarettes, a cigarette lighter and a shandy, or in the last few years a glass of port. Stucco remembers his grandmother sitting in the kitchen watching her husband, Stucco's grandfather, watching westerns on the television in the darkened living-room.

The evil cattle baron turns to look at Stucco and says: Hey, Stucco. There's such a thing as too much suspense.

Filming starts at six every morning. At six-thirty a band of outlaws ride into town. Stucco kills them all, his gun firing a hail of blanks, and then the outlaws are buried in the town cemetery, beneath Styrofoam tombstones that fall over in a light breeze. Some mornings he turns up late, and the outlaws have taken over and killed all the townspeople before he makes it to the set.

The supply of outlaws is small. He recognises each of them now, the same faces, the same dead bodies. Some of them are as tired as he is. To relieve the boredom, they devise increasingly spectacular deaths for themselves:

they fall from rooftops onto spiked fences, or get dragged screaming along the ground behind their horses with a foot tangled in the stirrups. Their death throes have become more noisy and violent, and the acting more hammy.

Stucco could go on like this indefinitely, but sooner or later the railway will arrive, and with it will come civilisation and the end of the Age of Heroes. His time will be up. He has to do something to redeem himself before the railway arrives.

A nose is a tiny appendage that weighs no more than a little finger and its only function is to act as a protective covering and as a filter for two small orifices. If the eyes are the windows to the soul, then the nose is the combined awning and fly screen. A nose is not an attractive thing at the best of times. The least offensive noses are the least obtrusive. Perhaps an insurance assessor could place a value on the loss of a nose, but the value would certainly be lower than for almost any other organ. The nose's prominent position is the only reason that its absence is so noticeable.

Beauty lies in symmetry: the more symmetrical a face the more attractive its appearance. But the lack of a nose, a single organ occupying a central position on the face, is only ugly when reflected by the startling presence of noses on the faces of other people.

Stucco

The scene opens with an establishing shot of a man riding across a plain, heading towards the town. From the right edge of the screen a rifle barrel swings across and aims at the rider. The gun fires and the rider falls off the horse. The horse circles. The rider gets up, mounts the horse and continues his progress. The rifle fires again. This time the horse falls, bringing the rider down with it. The horse gets up, the rider gets up, the rider mounts the horse. The rifle fires and the man falls off the horse. The man stands up and the rifle barrel lowers and drops off-screen. The man mounts the horse and keeps riding.

The man is Stucco's double, his stunt double. He is Stucco's representative in the physical world, a payrolled crash test dummy who assumes the responsibility for any pain or physical difficulty that Stucco would otherwise have to suffer. But since Stucco's accident their relationship has changed. The symmetry between the two men has been broken, and while the people laugh when they see Stucco, no-one laughs when they see his double.

When Stucco sees his double his hand goes to his face, covering the place where his nose once rested.

Stucco's life has turned into a series of disconnected incidents, devoid of meaning or purpose:
>an expression here,
>a pause before turning a corner,

walking slowly along a street,
a hand reaching for a gun,
a tip of the hat.

The cast speak in Spanish and Italian and German and English, reciting sequences of numbers or prayers or recipes, knowing that the real dialogue will be written and dubbed in afterwards in at least as many different languages. Stucco spends more time in his trailer watching old westerns, looking for ideas and, perhaps, for direction. He is convinced that his double is making jokes about him to the rest of the crew, detailing every shortcoming and every mistake that Stucco has ever made, every failing that the double, in his special position, is privy to.

Some men can trust other men, but some men cannot even trust themselves. Stucco starts avoiding his double, but his double neither approaches him nor avoids him. To anyone on the set the double seems to be acting politely and reasonably. Stucco is starting to feel suspicious but he is going to play it innocent as far as it takes him.

A few days later there is a knock on Stucco's trailer door. Stucco attaches his nose, adjusts it in the mirror, then opens the door. His double is standing outside. The double says: Can I come in?

Stucco says: W-well sure. Come in. Come in.

They sit on either side of a fold-up card table. Stucco's breath smells of liquor.

The double says: We, the crew and I, we've come up with something new we want to try tomorrow.

Stucco says: Like what?

The double says: We've been thinking about a death scene. Your death. You'll be shot by an unseen assailant.

Stucco says: Wait a minute. No. You can't do that. It doesn't make any sense. The story has barely started.

The double says: But you can come back as a ghost, see? As an avenging angel.

Stucco says: No. No. I don't want to die.

The double says: Don't be such a girl. Shut up, you're embarrassing me.

Stucco says: No. I won't do it. I won't go along with it.

The double says: Well, the way I figure it, you don't have much choice. Either I do the scene for you or you do it yourself. Either way you end up dead.

Stucco thinks about this a little, then he says: It won't hurt, will it?

The double says: No, of course not. I know what I'm doing. I'm a professional, aren't I?

The set is watered down until the main street turns into soft mud. The crew have been getting things ready since early in the morning. The cameras are set up to cover the shot, Sam Peckinpah style, from several different angles and at several different film speeds.

The double is there, hanging back but watching intently. Stucco takes his shirt off. One of the stunt men passes Stucco a metal breastplate and helps him to strap it on. A thin but strong metal wire is attached to the harness on the breastplate, at a point in the middle of Stucco's back, and the wire is trailed out on the ground behind him.

Two squibs, condoms filled with fake blood, pieces of meat and a small explosive charge, are glued to the breastplate over Stucco's heart. The squibs are wired up to a control box in the saloon. The double and a couple of stunt men put on thick gloves and take hold of the wire attached to Stucco's back and get ready to pull. The double smiles while Stucco puts his shirt back on.

The double says: When the first charge goes off, go limp. We'll pull you back. You'll leave the ground for a couple of feet, then you'll land on your back in the mud. There's sawdust mixed in with the dirt, to make the landing softer. As long as you remember to go limp it won't hurt at all. Then the second charge will go off. Don't move any more after that.

Stucco doesn't have to fake the expression of terror on his face as he goes down. His expression is so perfect that they don't even bother to do another take.

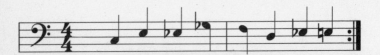

Courtesy Raymond Scott archive.

POWERHOUSE

In an unpublished letter, written in 1949, the American composer Raymond Scott described his vision of the future of music:

Nothing is impossible in this atomic age. As a composer who has dabbled for twenty years in 'sound acoustics', I wish the Einsteins of the world would focus their attention soon on the problem of accurate representation and reproduction of music . . . Some day, perhaps within the next hundred years, science will perfect a process of thought transference from composer to listener. Only by allowing the listener to see into the mind of the composer can the true value of the music be approximated.

Devices already have been perfected to record the impulses of the brain. In the music of the future, the composer will sit alone on the concert stage and merely think his idealised conception of his music. His brain waves will be picked up by mechanical equipment and channelled directly into the minds of his hearers, thus allowing no room for distortion of the original idea.

> Instead of recordings of actual music sound, recordings will carry the brain waves of the composer directly to the mind of the listener.

Raymond Scott was only partially successful in achieving his goal. By 1960, Raymond Scott had become an anonymous composer of advertising jingles and the recordings of the Raymond Scott Quintette were no longer available to the public. Only fragments of his music could still be heard, although their use was uncredited, in one hundred and seventeen of the cartoons produced by the Warner Brothers Studios between 1943 and 1962. Of these fragments, eight notes stand out: the piano riff at the beginning of the second section of the song 'Powerhouse'.

As a child I watched a lot of cartoons. I still watch a lot of cartoons. In the 1951 Warner Brothers cartoon *Early to Bet*, a cat and a bulldog are playing cards. The cat loses each hand. After each loss the dog says: 'You must pay the penalty,' and pulls out a vertically mounted gaming wheel from off-screen. 'Blues in the Night' plays as the cat spins the wheel; when the wheel stops the cat starts screaming 'No, not the *Post*. Not the *Post*,' or the name of the penalty the wheel has stopped on. The riff from 'Powerhouse' starts to play as the dog subjects the cat to the home-made torture device chosen by the penalty wheel. As the cartoon progresses, the penalties become progressively more violent and the riff from 'Powerhouse' becomes more intense.

Raymond Scott's real name was Harry Warnow. He picked the name Raymond Scott out of the Manhattan telephone book. In 1936 he formed the six-member Raymond Scott Quintette – he said that the word 'quintette' had a crisp sound – and between 1937 and 1939 his recordings sold millions of copies. After the band had broken up, several of the musicians from the Quintette complained that Scott had treated them like machines. Dorothy Collins, Scott's second wife, made similar complaints.

'Powerhouse' is playing on the stereo next to my desk. I have the CD player set so that 'Powerhouse' plays repeatedly. The stereo is in a cabinet to my left. A telephone shaped like Pac-Man is also to my left, on the desk. On my right, a little further from my desk, are several tall bookshelves. The bookshelves are filled with books, and the excess books are stacked on top of the bookshelves and in piles on the floor all around me. In front of me is the computer on which I am typing. Most of my time is spent sitting here at my desk.

I live in a two-bedroom flat; one of the bedrooms is used as the study and this is the room I am currently sitting in. Most of the flat is filled with papers and books, and every flat surface is covered with things that I have collected:

Pez dispensers,
Kinder Surprise toys,
Rubik's Cubes,
Godzilla figures,
Nintendo Game and Watches,
Happy Drinking Birds,
Viewmaster viewers,

sound toys,
Etch-A-Sketches of various sizes and types,
inflatable cows,
easy-listening records,
food packaging,
old postcards,
Diana cameras,
musical equipment,
Japanese replica food,
bath toys,
advertising figures,
Wombles,
snowdomes and so on.

I spend a lot of time collecting things, **a tendency not unknown in my family.** My father's father, who died when I was very young, collected steam engines and tractors, and was the owner of the only steam tractor made by the Cowlie factory of Ballarat. The collection was broken up and sold at auction after his death; the Cowlie tractor was bought by the Melbourne Museum. I still remember the sight of these **great machines** standing idle in the back paddock like grazing monsters.

I have been living here alone for the past seven weeks. Living alone does not suit me. When I am alone in the flat I dwell on every stupid thing I have ever done, either recently or in the past, back to and including the time that I accidentally addressed my teacher as 'Mother' in grade six. Since every stupid thing I have ever done involved other people, I usually decide that I am not very good at dealing with people and should avoid them in future.

Courtesy Raymond Scott archive.

I also drink a lot of coffee. I am aware that coffee distorts my perception, to the point where I view people who do not drink coffee (and, for different reasons, vegetarians) with a certain amount of distrust. The coffee also makes me urinate frequently. So: I get up in the morning and turn on the coffee machine in the kitchen and then the computer in the study. The rest of the day I walk between the kitchen and the study or between the study and the bathroom. At eleven-thirty in the morning I go downstairs and walk past the rest of the flats to get to the mailbox. On many days the mail does not arrive until four in the afternoon, so on those days I check the mailbox five or six times. If the mailbox is empty I make exaggerated gestures of disappointment, so that if anyone is watching me from one of the other flats I will look as if I am expecting something important.

I would be lying if I said that I did not wake up each morning without feeling a certain amount of distress.

In February 1995, I bought a CD containing the first available release in almost fifty years of the music of the Raymond Scott Quintette. I noticed the cover art first: a sleepwalker, a cigar-store Indian with a tommy gun, a pygmy holding an ice-cream cone containing the severed head of a missionary; all three figures are standing on a conveyor belt, and all are drawn in the style of a thirties cartoon. The cover blurb says: 'The Looney Melodies of the Man Who Made the Cartoons Swing', but it was the title, *Powerhouse*, which immediately formed the link in my mind between the CD I was holding and the eight notes that had so often played in my mind since earliest childhood.

Courtesy Raymond Scott archive.

Raymond Scott's widow, Mitzi, claims that Scott never watched cartoons, and had never seen the Warner Brothers cartoons that used his music. Scott was contracted to Twentieth-century Fox in 1938, seven months after the Quintette's first radio broadcast. Scott left Twentieth-century Fox after a year, complaining that 'they think everything is wonderful'.

When I turn up the volume of the stereo, the music becomes loud enough to stop me from dwelling on my problems. However, this introduces new problems. There are certain pieces of music, generally of a repetitive nature, that fill me with emotions of great violence. Even if I hear them in my mind I become slightly hysterical. Among these pieces are sections of the Introduzione of Bartók's 'Concerto for Orchestra', Varèse's 'Ionisation' and, most powerfully, the second section of Raymond Scott's 'Powerhouse'. I begin to think that if I listen to 'Powerhouse' too long something will happen to me. I could try to describe this feeling in my own words, but I could do no better than to quote a sentence from 'The Artushof', written by E.T.A. Hoffmann in 1815:

A well-known professor of physics has given it as his opinion that the Universal Spirit, bold experimenter that it is, has somewhere or other constructed a thoroughly efficient electrical machine, from which there run cunningly hidden wires; these wires extend throughout all of life and, elude them as we may, sooner or later we step on one; a lightning bolt then blasts its way through us – and suddenly everything has acquired a new shape.

Shortly after I bought that first CD of Raymond Scott's music I began to correspond with the man who had produced the CD: Irwin Chusid, a disc jockey for a New York radio station. Irwin first heard the name of the man responsible for 'Powerhouse' in 1989, when a friend mailed him a cassette tape of Raymond Scott's music recorded from old 78 rpm discs. Irwin found Scott in Van Nuys, living with his third wife, Mitzi. Raymond Scott was eighty-one years old. He had suffered a series of strokes, and was no longer able to speak.

When I first heard of Raymond Scott, in February 1995, he had been dead for only a year.

Raymond Scott called his work descriptive music. For now it will be sufficient to list the titles of some of his songs:
- 'Girl at the Typewriter',
- 'Boy Scout in Switzerland',
- 'War Dance for Wooden Indians',
- 'Twilight in Turkey',
- 'Bumpy Weather over Newark',
- 'Reckless Night on Board an Ocean Liner',
- 'New Year's Eve in a Haunted House',
- 'Confusion Among a Fleet of Taxicabs upon Meeting with a Fare',
- 'Dedicatory Piece to the Crew and Passengers of the First Experimental Rocket Express to the Moon',

'The Toy Trumpet' and
'Dinner Music for a Pack of Hungry Cannibals'.

Around the time of Raymond Scott's death I became sick and was unable to leave my bed for over a month. Shortly after I recovered I suffered a series of setbacks which, in retrospect, affected me more than I had expected. I lost the confidence I once had, and I became subject to fears and worries that I had never noticed before, feelings that began to intrude upon my daily existence.

I began to think that I would like to live in a world without individual people. As the sole survivor of some apocalypse, I could live surrounded only by the things that people had made and not by the people themselves. Or I could spend my life as a man in the crowd, an anonymous and unnoticed mass following a trajectory dictated solely by the flow of other people.

One of the things I most like about cartoons is that the emotions expressed by the characters are almost completely limited to the emotions that can be shown on the face. The animator, by the careful positioning of a few lines, can convey a simple range of feelings that, although few in number, are unambiguous and perfectly adequate for the kinds of situations that a cartoon character encounters.

The day follows the usual course. I drink too much coffee, and my hands begin to tremble and my heart beats

Courtesy Raymond Scott archive.

with a caffeine-induced arrhythmia. I feel like I am on the edge of panic. I can no longer sit down and I can no longer listen to Raymond Scott's 'Powerhouse'.

The city is only fifteen minutes away from my flat by tram. As I walk around the city, surrounded by a mass of anonymous people, I feel a pleasant sense of disconnection, as if I am looking at the world through a telescope.

The amount of variety I see in the physical characteristics of lumpen humanity always surprises me. While I am in the city I can wander aimlessly or follow people whose peculiarities of appearance or gait I find particularly interesting. I am free of the restrictions of the flat, my compulsive visits to the mailbox and to the coffee machine, with the ensuing demands on my bladder.

This pleasant feeling lasts for as long as I am not approached by anyone, either someone I know or someone who has decided that they must say something to me. I am aware that my own appearance is in some ways exceptional. I have what I have been told is a friendly face. With a certain regularity I am approached by people who either ask me what I am so happy about, or tell me how good it is to see such a happy person.

When someone approaches me, I am so surprised by the intrusion that I cannot think of anything to say.

Courtesy Raymond Scott archive.

My mood changes after my anonymity has been disturbed, and I start to think about returning to the flat. The tram ride back to the flat is always less pleasant than the trip in. I look out the windows at the passing buildings, to reduce the risk that someone will try to start up a conversation with me. Back at the flat I know the CD player is still running.

In the seat across from me, a woman is talking loudly to a man. She says: 'I've been working on my arm. It wouldn't come out, since the accident, but I've got it to go some. They never thought it would work at all.'

The man nods.

She continues on with a story about how another patient tried to rape her. The man does not seem to understand what she is talking about. He has greying hair and he wears ill-matching clothes and a child's baseball cap. The man's mouth hangs open. In one corner of his mouth is a pink conical object. I cannot determine whether it is a growth or a piece of food, and I watch intently, waiting for him to close his mouth, or lick his lips, to see if the object can be dislodged. After a few minutes I turn back to the view outside.

The tram turns at the top of Bourke Street, passes the Princess Theatre and the Surgeon's College and then continues up Nicholson Street toward the Exhibition Buildings. I could have travelled by the same route sixty years ago, when Raymond Scott was at the height of his popularity. Until 1940 the trams were propelled by cables and not electricity. A cable was mounted in a channel under the surface of the road, between the tracks. The cable

was driven by steam engines housed in buildings situated at the mid-point of each line.

On the line that I travel the old engine house is still standing, at the corner of Nicholson and Gertrude Streets. This is where the tram turns off Nicholson Street, the mid-point of my trip. I watch the building closely as the tram approaches the engine house, and I realise that 'Powerhouse' has started to play in my mind. The building has no exterior signage or features to reveal the purpose for which the building is now used. The windows are frosted, and no sign of movement or activity within can be seen from the outside. But I know the building is occupied, because at night I have seen an orange light coming from within.

Under the street, in front of the engine house, was a chamber containing a number of pulleys to divert the cable inside the building. Inside, a Babcock and Wilcox boiler provided the steam to drive the engines. A piston attached to the steam engine spun two drive wheels, one of which was ten feet and the other twenty-four feet in diameter. The cable passed around the drive wheels in a figure-of-eight, then around a tensioning wheel at the end of an eight-foot race. The heat generated by the machinery was considerable; inside the building the workers planted ferns that thrived in the heat and moisture, and grew to great heights. The machinery was noisy, audible from outside of the building, and the cable itself made a humming noise as it travelled the length of the tram line, perhaps the same broken chord that opens the song 'Powerhouse'.

The conductor sees me watching the building as we

go past and sits down next to me. She says: 'They give us a really hard time, you know. The whole line is controlled from in there. They can check the location of every tram, and if a tram is running late or early they buzz the driver to get him to go faster or go slower. Bastards. They make our lives a living hell.'

I say: 'The age of electricity began with the invention of the telegraph, the first device to allow instantaneous communication over a great distance. At the time the telegraph must have seemed like a magical device, powered by an invisible force. We still get a shock when we hear a machine try to speak to us: the sound of a ringing phone can fill us with emotions of great happiness or feelings of great fear and dread. The clicking of the telegraph key must have seemed like a communication from an incorporeal spirit, a reminder of the technique of table-rapping practised during seances by Victorian spiritualists trying to receive a message from the spirit world, the tapping out of words from the dead.'

On one of my many recent visits to the mailbox I received a package, sent to me by Irwin Chusid, containing material from the Raymond Scott archive. Inside the envelope were a collection of articles either about or by Raymond Scott, dating back to the thirties, and a series of glossy, eight-by-ten black-and-white photographs.

The photographs are in a pile on my desk. There are nine photographs in total, and I have arranged them in what I imagine to be chronological order. In the first

Courtesy Raymond Scott archive.

photograph Scott is sitting behind a piano, smiling and looking away from the camera. Next to him is a microphone bearing the CBS logo. Scott graduated from the Institute of Musical Art, later renamed the Juilliard School, in 1931, and was hired as the staff pianist for the CBS radio house band by his brother, Mark Warnow, who was the conductor.

The second photograph shows Scott with the members of the Quintette, sitting on folding metal chairs in a plain room, perhaps a rehearsal room. After five years at CBS Scott became bored. He persuaded the CBS producer Herb Rosenthal to let him form his own group, the Quintette, to play his original compositions.

The third photograph shows the Quintette playing in a concert hall. In 1939 the Quintette was given a record contract by the Master label, and was very successful. The next photograph, clearly a posed publicity shot, I imagine to have been taken during this period in Scott's life. Scott sits behind a piano. On the piano is a microphone, and beside the piano is a table. On the table is a blank sheet of music paper and an eraser. Scott has his left hand over the piano keys, and in his right hand he holds a pencil. But Scott never used written scores – he composed only on the Quintette. The musicians were expected to memorise their parts after Scott played them himself on the piano. Scott would not allow improvisation. His players had to strictly follow his arrangements. Scott said that written scores inhibited players, but at the same time he allowed his musicians no freedom at all.

Courtesy Raymond Scott archive.

The fifth photograph shows Scott wearing headphones and smiling broadly. In front of him is what I imagine to be a machine for making recordings on metal or acetate discs. Scott recorded every performance and every rehearsal.

The sixth photograph shows Scott, jacketless and standing, striking a tympanum with mallets. His expression is serious. On the wall behind him are painted flowing musical staves, two treble clefs and a packet of Lucky Strike cigarettes. The photograph could be from 1943 when, for a few months, he was on the radio program *Broadway Bandbox*, sponsored by Lucky Strike cigarettes. A Raymond Scott composition would alternate with a number sung by Frank Sinatra. The two did not get along and Scott soon left the show. But the photograph is probably from 1949, the year Scott recorded his vision of the future of music and the year his brother Mark died. Scott replaced him as band leader of the Lucky Strike Orchestra on *Your Hit Parade*.

The seventh photograph is of Scott at home, sitting on his bed wearing a casual check shirt and talking on the telephone. I would have placed this photograph earlier: his face is soft and unlined, and his close-cropped hair makes him look young, perhaps around my age. But on the shelf above the bed is a stack of Popular Science magazines and a book labelled *The American Annual of Photography 1949*, making him at least forty-one. His natural pose and expression make me believe that the photograph is not staged.

In the eighth photograph Raymond Scott is leaning over the open casing of an electronic device with a soldering iron in his hand. Behind him is a large upright metal case, with various knobs and dials on its facing side, and in the foreground is a console with covered with terminals and knobs. This photograph is from the second part of Scott's career. During the late forties Scott began building his own electronic instruments. In 1948 he built the Karloff, a machine that could imitate a chest cough, kitchen clatter, the sizzle of a frying steak and jungle drums. He built a keyboard called the Clavivox that simulated the sound of a Theremin. In 1960 Scott designed the first musical pitch sequencer, but by then Scott had withdrawn from the outside world, working in secret and refusing to let any but his closest associates know about his machines.

The last photograph contains no people at all, only an instrument that Raymond Scott designed and built from 1958 and 1970, the year I was born. Scott called the instrument the Electronium. Two Electroniums were built, although the second was probably constructed from the cannibalised remains of the first. The instrument is shaped like a large desk with a three-panelled console on top. The side consoles are angled toward the middle of the desk, and the front panels are covered with lights and switches, like the controls of an aircraft, and glow with an orange light. Scott called the instrument a *cockpit of dreams*, and gave it the power to compose music by itself.

METHOD OF OPERATION

A composer asks the Electronium to *suggest* an idea – theme – motive – whatever. He listens to these on a monitor speaker. When happy with one of the ideas, he stops the Electronium, puts the magnetic tape recorder into the record mode and starts recording. The start button for the Electronium is now also pressed and the composition is underway.

Say the opening theme is just about over, the composer (guidance control) decides that, as the first step in the development of his theme – he wishes to repeat it, but in a higher key – for instance, to widen some of the intervals . . . he turns another knob. Whatever the composer needs . . . to continue the development of the piece, it is but necessary for him to convey his wishes to the Electronium – by manipulating the appropriate controls.

. . . faster, slower, a new rhythm design, a hold, a pause, a second theme, variation, an extension, elongation, diminution, counterpoint, a change in phrasing, an ornament . . . ad infinitum . . . whatever the composer requests, the Electronium accepts and acts out his directions.

A while ago I started collecting photographs of tin toys which reminded me of Raymond Scott's compositions. I would collect the toys themselves, but tin toys of an appropriate vintage have become popular with collectors and are too expensive these days. I have a photograph of a toy trumpet, a rocketship, a wind-up penguin, an ocean liner, an aircraft, a yellow taxi, a toy drum and several others. By arranging them in different ways I hope to discern some pattern that will lead me to a satisfactory solution. I make room on my desk and lay them all out where I can see them.

Courtesy Raymond Scott archive.

I pick up one photograph, of a tin-plate battery-operated toy made by the Masutoku toy factory in the sixties. The caption on the photograph reads:

Bear the Typist is the name of this jolly little Japanese battery toy. Seated at an office desk, the bear starts operating her typewriter until she is interrupted by the ringing of the telephone. She picks it up, answers it with a few squeaks, replaces it and carries on with her work.

My own phone rings: I let the answering machine take the call. Habits soon become routines, and the days pass with a mechanical rhythm for as long as the batteries last. I need some sort of guidance. I wait for the lightning to blast through me, but nothing happens. Nothing is going to happen for as long as I sit here at my desk.

I believe that Raymond Scott's life had a single goal. His earliest experiments in thought transference were conducted on the Quintette. But the failure of mechanical techniques – torturous, endless rehearsals intended to make the musicians reproduce Scott's ideas perfectly – and the inconsistent and imprecise behaviour of his human machines, forced him to abandon this approach.

I struggle to write these words. I cannot hope for my thoughts to reach you in any but the most dilute form. But I am no engineer, and I must use the only methods available to me, methods that you despised.

Then he divided his task into two stages. First Scott built the Electronium, a machine he must have believed

Powerhouse

Courtesy Raymond Scott archive.

could be engineered to contain his own thoughts. For what other reason would he give the machine an amount of independence that he would not give to a human musician? The second stage would have been the design of a machine to accurately reproduce these thoughts in another human being. But before the first stage was completed Raymond Scott suffered a stroke, the first of a series of lightning bolts that left him without the ability to speak.

I am not sure what I expect to see inside the powerhouse. I can think of only three alternatives: machinery as high as the ceiling, the great wheels and the ferns and the intolerable heat; banks of consoles glowing with an orange light; or an empty room. I am frightened by the thought that I will find an empty room.

    I knock on the door of the powerhouse and wait. A man with a handlebar moustache opens the door, dressed in the green uniform of the Public Transport Corporation. He looks at me.　　　　I hope to recognise his face, but there is nothing familiar about him. I try to say something to the man standing in the doorway of the powerhouse, but I am unable to speak.　　　　I feel a sharp pain in my head. The man looks at me as if I am a drug addict or one of the homeless insane people that I myself often watch as I walk around the city. After a while he closes the door. I stand there, unsure of what I should do.

I catch the first tram that comes. I don't notice which direction the tram is going. I am sure that I can hear the cable humming beneath the tram. When I enter the flat I turn on the coffee machine and then the computer, in that order. The phone rings but I let the answering machine take the call.

Scott said that the Electronium was like a typewriter that wrote the story itself. I no longer know who wrote this story, whether it was me or Raymond Scott. But Raymond Scott can no longer speak. There is nothing more that I can say.

The Chicken Holocaust

TINTOOKI FROGS

We left Melbourne on a Saturday morning and headed north along the Calder Highway. We had no destination in mind, but we still felt like we were on a mission, as if in some inverted version of *On the Road*.

On the floor pan of the front passenger seat was a Japanese Tiger-brand thermos filled with Brazilian coffee. In the car stereo was a cassette tape of Pérez Prado's easy-listening mambo hits. On the back seat was a doona, two computers, and a book about the spaghetti westerns of Sergio Leone. We forgot to bring pillows.

We stopped at each tourist trap we came across, and we left each of them with a handful of brochures for other, similar locations. Most of them were disappointingly generic:

> bland antique shops and gift shops selling fake Victoriana and reproduction Early Settler furniture,
> golliwogs renamed 'gollies',
> scented soap and candles,
> clumsy pottery,
> ugly jumpers made from alpaca hair,

paintings of gum trees and old tin sheds,
bottles of essential oils,
crystals,
opals,
aromatherapy cures,
meditation books and
other New Age crap.

In Castlemaine we found an antique shop selling LPs for two dollars each. We bought a double-album set of the Enoch Light Orchestra playing the *Big Hits of the Seventies* in quadraphonic sound ('Fabulous for dancing! Marvellous for listening!'); a 1979 K-Tel greatest hits compilation called *Full Boar*, featuring a photograph of a severed pig's head wearing sunglasses and bulky headphones on the cover; the *Let a Frown Be Your Umbrella* LP by Oscar the Grouch on the Sesame Street label; *Party Sing Along with Mrs Mills*; and *Play it Again* by the Alan Gardiner Accordion Band.

A little past Harcourt we stopped at a combination cool-store and junk shop and bought some Red Fuji apples. In the carpark was a billboard that read:

Tintooki Frogs
**Hop in and help
the handicapped**
5KM ON THE LEFT

I said: 'This could be what we're looking for.'

By the time we had seen the place it was too late to stop, and the special logic of road trips, learned in childhood, demanded that we could not turn back. Tintooki Frogs was hidden behind some trees at the end of an overpass. It was a small cottage with a high-peaked corrugated-iron roof painted yellow and an Australian flag on a flagpole attached to the front verandah. The name 'Tintooki Frogs' was painted on the roof in large green letters. Next to it was a BP service station.

We kept driving until we reached the outskirts of Bendigo. We stopped at a warehouse selling second-hand office furniture, reconditioned glass-fronted refrigerators, old computer terminals and printers, an airport X-ray machine and an assortment of used medical equipment. I bought two auriscopes and stole a third. We should have bought some kidney trays as well, to use as snack dishes when we have visitors.

A couple of blocks from the warehouse we took some photographs of a takeaway restaurant called the BBQ Chicken Ranch. Painted on the side wall was a pink, plucked cartoon chicken, dragging a cooked chicken on a tray behind him. The cartoon chicken was looking back at the cooked chicken with a scared expression and sweat was dripping from its face, either from exertion or fear, as if this was a depiction of the Chicken Holocaust.

It was late in the afternoon. We booked into a thirty-five-dollar-a-night caravan park near the city centre. The caravan was reasonably clean, but in the caravan park's communal bathroom I had to pass four toilet cubicles in a row before I found one that had been flushed.

We unpacked the car and then drank our coffee. Children were playing in the adventure playground across from us. Some of the caravans had double carports that held two cars each, mainly customised Monaros and V8 Ford Fairlanes. Several caravans had small gardens of potted plants surrounded by foot-high white picket fences and vinyl awnings to protect the ageing inhabitants from the sun while they sat outside on plastic garden chairs.

After dark we drove into the centre of Bendigo and parked the car. Then we walked around for a while, trying to find somewhere to eat that looked cheap. We were alone except for a car full of teenage boys who honked each time they drove past us. After eight laps they gave up.

We ate a counter meal at the Old Crown Hotel. I had a good steak with vegetables and chips for seven dollars. A hen's party was in progress: five young women, wearing tuxedos and false moustaches, and an older woman who was probably the bride's mother. The hen's party was very quiet. I asked the waitress if the hotel had rooms available. She told me it was twenty-five dollars for a double room, including breakfast. I only mention this because it seems like a good deal.

We were back at the caravan park and in bed by eight-thirty. The mattress was thin and had a plastic cover, which was cold and uncomfortable. We sat up in bed and looked through our collection of brochures, marking the places we wanted to visit the next day.

Our trip would have made more sense twenty years ago, when we were still kids and tourism was a cottage industry, the product of the dreams and obsessions of individuals rather than the market research departments of large corporations. The modern tourist does not want to experience a proprietor's *personal vision*. The modern tourist travels to *get away from it all*, to feel nostalgia for a gentler, quieter age, when everything had either a rustic charm or an ornate splendour and life was uncomplicated, or else they go to Warner Brothers Movie World because the kids pestered them into it.

The roadside attractions of my childhood, filled with wonderful collections of junk and cheap plastic knick-knacks, are disappearing. Their proprietors, like Kerouac's hobos and Sergio Leone's gunfighters, are the last of a dying race.

The next morning we left Bendigo, following the directions given by one of the tourist brochures to get to Sandhurst Town. The ad copy said that Sandhurst Town was 'The Attraction with Something for Everyone':

Street Theatre brings the Gold Rush Alive. Gold Wash Gully diggings is a two-acre stage for the most entertaining street theatre you've ever experienced. You'll meet Digger Dan, Generous George the storekeeper and the loathsome Gold Commissioner.

There was also supposed to be a train called the Red Rattler, a General Store ('the Home of Fair Dinkum Eucy Oil'), and a once-monthly re-enactment of the Red Ribbon Rebellion.

At the end of the track where we expected Sandhurst Town to be, we found a Buddhist retreat and meditation centre. The Buddhists had put up a sign saying, 'No Entry to Sandhurst Town', so we turned around and kept looking.

We searched for over an hour before we gave up and returned to Bendigo. We bought pancakes at an ice-cream parlour that stuck little Australian flags, glued to toothpick flagpoles, in the middle of everything they served. We told the waitress that we had been trying to find Sandhurst Town. She told us that Sandhurst Town had been doing badly, and had closed a couple of months before. The property had been turned into a Buddhist retreat.

The rest of the morning we visited markets and junk shops and pottery studios. At the carpark of the Epsom Market we paid some Girl Guides four dollars to wash the car. They did a terrible job.

We started back for Melbourne in the early afternoon. From a roadside winery we bought two bottles of apple cider that tasted like homebrew. The owner told us that times were bad. People had stopped coming up from Melbourne. I asked him why. He blamed the drought.

From this direction, Tintooki Frogs was easy to spot. We parked out in front. The door of the cottage was closed, so we went into the service station and asked to see the frogs. A young man took us to the cottage and unlocked the front door. We each paid him the three-dollar entry fee. He walked in ahead of us and turned on a tape recorder. 'The Rainbow Connection' started to play, and the young man followed us around the place, singing along with Kermit the Frog. The young man's name was Damon, but his adoptive mother, Margot Archibald, called him *the handicapped boy*.

I cannot describe thirteen thousand frogs in eleven hundred words. The cottage itself is a single room. There is a counter along one wall, next to the front door, and the rest of the room is lined with glass-fronted display cases filled with frogs:

ceramic frogs,

Copperart frogs,

plastic frogs,

earthenware frogs,

a whole shelf of frog-shaped salt and pepper shakers,

wooden hand-carved Balinese frogs,

frog spoons,

empty Kermit the Frog-shaped shampoo bottles,

a fake Fabergé egg containing a crystal-cut frog,

a frog-in-a-box,

gemstone frogs,

a frog riding a Vespa,

a frog in a Volkswagen Beetle,

a frog-inspired teapot,

frog-shaped soaps,

an inflatable frog-shaped paddling pool,

a frog dressed as Santa Claus,

frogs in cowboy outfits,

frog earrings and other frog jewellery,

frogs in tuxedos with bow ties, top hats and cigars.

Margot Archibald started the collection because Damon's natural mother had hated frogs. When Margot adopted Damon she decided that she would teach him to love frogs. 'It started as a bit of a joke', she said, 'but it became a mania after a while.'

At the rear of the cottage is a doorway that leads to the back verandah. On the back verandah is a row of shelves covered with frogs:

frog castanets,

frogs made of seashells with glued-on googly eyes,

frog fridge magnets,

frogs having a tea party,

frog-shaped lanterns made of tin,

plastic swimming frog bath toys,

winking frogs,

worried-looking frogs and

frog planters made from cane.

'They are all mine,' Margot said. 'I've done every frog. I know every frog in the house. There's over thirteen thousand and it's the biggest collection in the world. I've had the French Collectables out here, and they think this is the best collection of anything they've ever seen. It's been written up. I've got the big magazine up there, a coloured magazine, and I've got the whole page – Margot and her frogs. I was just getting it going well and I had to go and have a car accident and be crippled for the rest of my life. I don't know what I'm going to do with it yet. I'm not going to split it – I hope not to. I want to live up the back, and I want to keep this going if I can.

'We've got a lot of work to be done here. I can't do much at all now after losing my husband. I've not long buried him. He just went suddenly, dropped dead. I died three times in St Vincent's last year. They said I'd never survive the accident, but I'm still going, and I'm older than my husband was.'

Since the accident, Margot was confined to a **three-wheeled Fisher & Paykel scooter.** She could no longer maintain the place. The scooter was too difficult to manoeuvre in confined spaces, and Margot could not afford to hire someone to clean and dust. As a result, the frogs were getting dusty and falling into disarray. Sometimes visitors even stole frogs.

Behind the cottage is a prefabricated steel shed filled with frogs:

> huge velveteen-covered frogs,
> frogs playing guitars,
> frogs carrying umbrellas,
> see-no-evil hear-no-evil speak-no-evil frogs,
> plush adult-sized Kermit the Frogs,
> frog compositions in metal,
> a Chinese frog shrine,
> concrete frog garden ornaments,
> frogs in matching bride and groom outfits with a frog priest in attendance,
> a frog beanbag,
> a Prince Charming frog,
> gumshoe frogs,
> gumnut frogs,
> a happy frog holding a sign that says 'I'm so happy I could just croak'.

'I like making it look nice. It's all me in those, I just love them. This place was built for the frogs. I don't know if I'll be able to get someone to keep it going at this stage.'

As she turned the scooter it began to beep like a reversing truck. Gurgling sounds came from a pair of fish tanks: bubbles of air released from the opening and closing mouths of an assortment of frog-shaped tank ornaments.

'I arranged everything. That's what the French Collectables people liked about it. They reckon that most collections they see are just everything in a straight line, and it's not even attractive. They've got all spoons or sugar basins or rabbits, but they haven't got them arranged nicely.' She hoped to get the *Guinness Book of Records* people out to count the frogs.

A path leads up from the cottage to a room called the Kelly House, at the back of the service station. A Mr Kelly made many of the frogs in this room himself, sculpting their wooden forms with a chainsaw. The room is filled with frogs:

> frogs sitting around a dining table,
> frogs sitting on the sideboard,
> a frog on a penny farthing bicycle,
> frogs playing basketball,
> a waist-high Toad of Toad Hall,
> a frog-theme tea towel,
> a Freddo Frog beach towel,
> a transparent plastic shower curtain with frogs painted
>   on it hanging from the wall.

Mr Kelly, Margot told us, had since gone blind.

'We don't get near enough tourists as we should. It's hard to see, and the council won't let me put signs up. They say because it's only a frog collection . . . they don't appreciate it for what it is. A lot of locals have never seen it. I had an estate agent out here the other day and he couldn't believe it. He said: "I've lived here all the years you've been here, and I had no idea it was like this." He said: "This is unreal."'

Cars pulled up outside, bought petrol, and drove off again. No-one came in to look at the frogs. I tried to imagine what they would think of the place: the old women in curlers, the local hoodlums in their V8 utes, the Melbourne businessmen with their blonde wives and designer-clothed kids out on a day trip. Most of them would have their own little collections, stamps or silver spoons or baseball cards or heavy metal albums, which they would accrue half-heartedly and sooner or later discard.

Margot said: 'I don't know what's going to happen when the new highway comes in. We'll only get traffic going one way, and I don't know how that is going to affect us. So I don't know what I'm going to do, but they are beautiful, aren't they?'

I looked around at the frogs and the frogs looked back. They looked pretty happy to me.

'Yes,' I said, 'they are beautiful.'

SALARYMAN

It's a hard world for little things.

Night of the Hunter

DAY ONE

I never wanted to be a Salaryman. The only thing I ever wanted to be was the guy who wore the Godzilla suit and got to stomp all over a miniature Tokyo. But things have been quiet in the mascot business. I need the money.

It starts like this: I am sitting at home watching *The Planet of the Apes* on video when I get a phone call. The head of the design department of an advertising agency is calling me, a company I did some freelance work with a few months before.

The boss says: 'Ip-dip-dog-shit-you-are-it.'

'I'm it?'

I am surprised by the offer. I hate the boss. We fought like children when I worked for him before, on a pitch for a large chain of toy retailers. Most days we had ended up throwing security cards at each other.

'I'm out of here. Find someone else to put up with your crap.'

'All right. You go home. *Go home*. We get someone else to finish job.'

'All right.'

'Good. Go home.'

'Right. Good luck.'

Then we would talk each other around and eventually I would take back my security card and go back to work. The boss is the most unpleasant, evil little man I have ever met, a completely incompetent Malaysian with no social skills and highly creative accounting practices. He always says: 'Keep it *crassy*.' I take *crassy* to mean a combination of crass and crappy.

But I need the money: the dishwasher broke down the week before. Being poor would be easy if things never broke down. The flat is already full of machines that no longer work but I cannot afford to replace them.

At an early age I realised that I lived in a world full of bad design. I had needed no leap of faith to conclude that I lived in a badly designed world.

'Bags I,' I say, sadly.

DAY TWO

I go into the office in the city centre. The building is a typical office building renovated in the mid-eighties. The building already looks dated. The foyer, lined with hairdressing salons and newsagents and gift shops, leads to a glass-roofed atrium ringed with elevator shafts. Filling the centre of the atrium is a stylised glass-and-steel garden in a shallow pool of water. I think there is something symbolic about it, but I couldn't guess what that might be. On the top floor, a floor above where I will be working, is a balcony where the executives eat lunch.

If one of them jumped off they would make a real mess.

I take the elevator to the penultimate floor and wait for the guard to let me in the security door. I follow him to the boss's office at one end of the building, separated from the rest of the workplace by a glass partition so he can watch work getting done.

I sit down and he offers me a three-month full-time contract, starting immediately. He tells me he will write up the contract when he gets the time. Until then I can invoice him weekly.

I feel the ghost of Samuel Goldwyn perch on my shoulder and whisper to me: *a verbal contract isn't worth the paper it's written on*. I try to think up some other ghost to balance the argument but I can't. The boss is pointing to a space behind me, past Samuel Goldwyn, through the glass partition, to a vacant cubicle in the middle of the floor.

I say: 'Uh yeah, right. I'll take the job. Thank you, Great Sage and Equal of Heaven.'

I go to my new cubicle, saying to myself: 'Stupid, stupid, stupid . . . He's paying you half of what you're worth and you've got nothing from him in writing. You don't even want a full-time job, you've never wanted a full-time job and you've never had a full-time job. You'll be lucky if you can last three weeks without going crazy.' I sit down on my new chair and switch on the computer on the desk in front of me. The partitions that make up the sides of my cubicle have happy faces printed on them. I start to draw a moustache on the face in front of me.

DAY THREE

I am a mouse jockey, employed to push a plastic rodent around a large rectangle of on-screen real estate. This morning I have a meeting with an art director who wants me to design some mock-ups for a print ad. He tries to explain the kind of look he wants. I tell him I have no idea what he is talking about and I tell him to come back to me when he has enough of an idea for me to do something with. Then we argue a bit, and I finally agree to do a mock-up, just to humour him.

I do a mock-up and show it to the art director. He tells me it looks nothing like what he wants, but I know that already. I know exactly what he wants but I am playing dumb, waiting for the whole little drama to reach its logical conclusion. An hour later I show him another mock-up which he also turns down, but instead of trying to

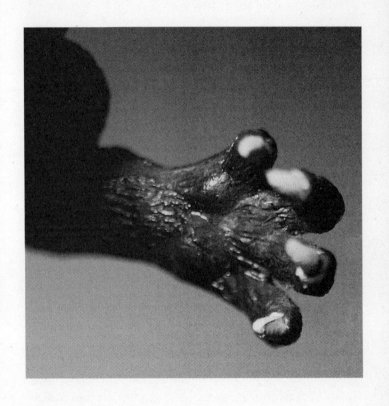

explain what he wants again he goes to his office and brings back a design magazine. He opens the magazine to a marked page and shows the page to me. He says: 'I want something like this.' I give him a big smile, so he knows that I know I beat him. He doesn't seem to notice.

He leaves the magazine with me, and I do a mock-up that looks exactly like the ad from the magazine, the ad he wanted me to rip off all along. I show it to him and he says: 'Good work. That's exactly what I wanted.'

I call this the Law of Second-hand Creativity. Like some misguided physicist I have decided to document the immutable laws that govern the workings of the corporate advertising universe. One day I will publish papers on my findings with titles like *How to be Slightly Innovative* and *What is it about Montage that Drives Clients Wild?* and *Leni Riefenstahl's Heritage: the Successful Use and Application of Fascist Imagery in Corporate Reports*.

After lunch I have a meeting with a couple of creative directors, and they brief me on a brochure for the tourism board of one of the northern states.

One of the creative directors gives me the sketches he has made for the title page of each section of the brochure. In the advertising business these people are just called *creatives*, but I prefer to use the full title. For the restaurant section the creative director has drawn the Aboriginal flag with a knife and fork added on either side of the central circle.

I say: 'Jesus, I can't use that.'
He says: 'Why not?'

I say: 'It's . . . kind of in bad taste.'

He says: 'Are you sure? I really liked it. I thought it was clever.'

I say: 'No. It's in bad taste. I'm *sure*.'

When I get back to my cubicle I start to wonder why I said anything. Nobody else would have noticed, including the clients, and I was unlikely to get blamed if they did. I should have kept quiet. The only fun to be had in a job like this was getting away with as much irony as possible without anybody noticing.

If I came up with a nightmare vision of out-of-control consumerism for a credit card company they would use it without hesitation. Clients suffer from a distinctive type of tunnel vision: every client believes that their product is the most important thing in the world, including advertising companies, which think that advertising is the most important thing in the world. Without fabric softener or moisturising cream or market research services they think the whole world would fall apart; maybe they're right, what the hell would I know.

DAY FOUR

All clients look the same: bloated white larval creatures in suits, with the exception of airline executives, who have tans. The buildings that surround the building I work in are the hives of these creatures, where workers toil under the direction of toadlike CEOs, stupid fat bastards who endlessly repeat meaningless phrases about innovation and empowered workers and improved market shares, as if the words were some kind of religious mantra. Part of my job is to make these creatures look presentable, to touch up their yellowed teeth and fogged, dull eyes and double-chins and skin complaints and superimpose them on scenes that could pass for out-takes from *Triumph of the Will*.

In normal circumstances the people in my department do not wear suits; the design department involves nominally creative behaviour and the clients feel more comfortable if they see us wearing normal clothes. When a designer starts wearing a suit it means that the designer's skills are so few or so poor that, rather than face unemployment, they are pushing for a managerial position. But once they start wearing a suit they can never go back, whatever the result.

I get a visitor, a stray suit from the marketing floor with nothing else to do. He talks to me while I work and I try to ignore him. He tells me we are lucky to be working in a creative business. He tells me about his new car. He tells me I am lucky to get to do such fun work.

I say: 'Let me tell you a little story. You like stories, Joe? This is a moral story, the Parable of Joe, the Market Researcher.

'Once upon a time there was a boy called Joe. Joe wasn't interested in anything, and had no skills or abilities, so inevitably Joe went into market research.

'A market researcher's job was to find out what the average schmuck wants, the sort of thing that appeals to the lowest common denominator. A lot of companies made a profit selling rubbish to schmucks: they realised that it was very important for them to know exactly what colour their rubbish should be or what it should smell like. So over time the marketing departments got bigger and bigger and bigger.

'Then one day Joe said: "Hey, why do we do all this research to find out what the lowest common denominator wants? We *are* the lowest common denominator. We can rule the world!"

'This was the first and last time a market researcher had a thought. Since then, the world has been ruled by marketing schmucks.

'But you see Joe, this story makes me wonder. Who is the real schmuck here, you or me? You see Joe, this story wasn't really a parable. It was a true story. See, some people believe in what is and others believe in what should or could be. I believe in what might as well be, and if everybody shared my belief we could all avoid a lot of confusion.

'Do you get me, Joe?'

DAY FIVE

I am never going to make it as a Salaryman. I don't even know what CEO stands for, or what *liaising* means. I have never worked full-time in an office before and I am having a lot of trouble getting into character. I say things I know I am not supposed to say but I can't stop myself. I am never positive about anything when I know I am paid to be positive about everything. If an art director asks me for my opinion I refuse to give him one: how can I pick out the best layout from a selection of four if all of them are crap? How can I distinguish between four levels of mediocrity?

At times like this I think that I am incapable of proper social behaviour, that I am unable to meet the basic requirements of social interaction. Some people would get depressed by such thoughts, but I am always reassured by the belief that my failure has a biological basis. When I was a kid I read an article in a popular science magazine that, although only half-remembered, I often tell people about, filling in the forgotten details with my own conclusions and the results of my own experiments.

When fish first crawled out of the sea and became reptiles they had small brains with only a limited range of functions. Their brains contained only the most basic instincts: hunger, aggression and the urge to procreate. These urges make up all the functions of the reptile brain and are all a reptile needs to survive. I am a reptile, and reptiles are only concerned with the most immediate desire of each moment: fast-food commercials, colourful packaging and supermarkets all appeal to the reptile brain.

After millions of years, reptiles evolved into birds. In the process their brains got larger. The part of the brain shared by birds and reptiles didn't change: instead a new piece of brain grew around the reptile brain, like a rumpus room tacked onto the back of a suburban house. Although this annex is shared by all birds **I think it is appropriate to call it the chicken brain.** The chicken brain lives in constant fear and is always worrying about any potential threat to its existence. Superannuation schemes, health food, Nautilus equipment and conservative governments all appeal to the chicken brain.

To test these theories, the researchers in the article had taken a number of chickens and a number of a highly aggressive species of Mexican lizards and performed a series of experiments. Grafting bits of chicken brain onto the brains of Mexican lizards made the lizards docile and fearful, while grafting bits of lizard brain onto the brains of chickens made the chickens more aggressive and more sexually active. At this point I say that these experiments demonstrate more than the potential for breeding hyper-aggressive chickens.

When birds evolved into monkeys they grew another mental rumpus room, the monkey brain. The article had not discussed the properties of the monkey brain, but my recent experiences were giving me a good idea of how the monkey brain worked. I believed that the monkey brain was solely interested in monitoring and controlling the behaviour of others. I imagined that the monkey brain evolved to accommodate the social requirements of groups of primates, over-riding the more antisocial urges of the chicken and reptile brains. Management books, art appreciation classes and self-help books all appeal to the monkey brain.

I believe that human behaviour – of myself, my co-workers and the various executives I have to deal with – depends on the varying ratios of reptile, chicken and monkey brain matter that fill our skulls.

The first week is over. I have drawn moustaches,

glasses, scars and devil's horns on all of the faces on the walls of my partitions. I use a Stanley knife to slit their throats. The partition stuffing – used bandages from some Third World hospital – starts falling out on the floor.

I still haven't got a contract.

DAY EIGHT

I put in my first invoice. I had been thinking about the money all weekend. With overtime it comes to quite a large sum, more money than I sometimes have had to live on for more than a month. I started to experience an unexpected conflict between my chicken brain and my reptile brain. I began alternating between feelings of elation and dread. At one moment I am planning all the things I am going to buy with my new income and at the next I am worrying about spending it too fast or being fired for my *bad attitude*. I am worried that if I stay at this place too long my chicken brain will come to dominate my thoughts. Maybe settling down is an evolutionary process, but I have no confidence in evolution and I have no idea what the alternatives are.

The boss is a reptile like me. He is only pretending to be a monkey. The other bosses hate him, but he keeps a tight hold on the department and he keeps the rest of the bosses ignorant of its workings. Everything has to pass through the boss. The other bosses must think there is some skill, some special trick or a certain sympathy that is needed to run a design department, and leave him alone.

I have told you how I spend my days. I will tell you how the boss spends his. The boss arrives at work in the morning and goes straight into his office. He sits there for a while reading brochures and flipping through magazines. He could be sitting in someone else's waiting room. If anyone comes into the office he ignores them or gets rid of them as quickly as possible.

After a couple of hours he wanders out of his office and starts the next stage of his routine, which I call Management By Walking About. He passes each cubicle and looks at what each of us is working on. Then he makes suggestions, which means he tells us to do something other than what we are currently doing. He tells us to make the shadows darker, or to use another colour, or to 'tighten it up' but 'remember to keep it *crassy*'. He likes to fiddle with the knobs on my monitor and tells me how important it is to keep our monitors calibrated. He tells me my monitor is too bright or too dark and turns the contrast knob until he is happy, or he says the contrast is too high and turns down the brightness. And I sit there and agree with him, the same as I would agree with him if he told me two plus two equalled five. This is his only trick, keeping us all confused, the inhabitants of an arbitrary and cruel world without meaning or direction or purpose. He tells us to change something one way, then the next time he sees it he tells us to change it back. Then he tells us to change it again, until we can no longer trust our sensibilities or even our senses.

Then he goes back to his office and reads through the same brochures and flips through the same magazines. Once a month, when it comes time to balance the budget, he sacks someone, either because they are too old or too young or he doesn't like them or they work too hard or they don't work hard enough or he thinks they are too comfortable and need the fear of God put in them. He sacks them to balance the budget. He does whatever he can to keep the department confused because confusion is in his best interest: *something* will always get done, no matter how much he interferes or obstructs its progress, but if he ever stopped interfering someone might realise he isn't needed. The boss treats us like we are the fingers of his own hands. He presses down on us and we do what his own fingers lack the ability to do. Then, if a finger displeases him he can bite it off and just grow another finger. Things are that simple.

I am terrified that I will learn to live like this.

DAY NINE

Working full-time in an office is an offence against nature. I can cite several reasons: the air-conditioning dries up the mucous membranes in my nostrils, making me sneeze frequently and filling my nose with hard, crusty snot. My throat has dried up and my voice is becoming increasingly harsh. My shoulders and arms are cramped from pushing the mouse around all day and my mouse hand has curled up

into a permanent claw shape. The base of my spine aches at the tip of the coccyx, and I am convinced that this vestigial tail has been damaged by constant chair-sitting and has started to protrude the wrong way. The sedentary nature of the work means I am putting on weight, particularly on my hips and legs, and my forehead has worked itself into a permanent frown. Even my eyebrows are getting bushier.

I fall asleep at the keyboard and dribble into the keys. I dream that I walk into a nightclub and a girl hands me a CD with a picture of a penny-farthing bicycle on the case. She tells me the CD is complimentary. Along the walls of the nightclub are rows of silver-painted mannequins with stereo components built into their torsos. I check each mannequin but none of them have a CD player. I go back to the girl at the door and ask her if I can take the CD home to listen to. She says no, and tells me that they have the CDs melted down to recoup the cost of their manufacture. I ask her what is recorded on the CD, and she tells me there is nothing.

I wake up and look at the clock. It is one in the morning and the office is empty. I leave the building and walk to the taxi rank. I get in a taxi driven by a young man who talks like a particularly stupid surfer. He asks me if I have been at a party. I tell him I have been working. He asks me where I work and I tell him I work in an advertising agency.

He says: 'Is it like D & D Advertising?'

I say I have never heard of that company.

He says: 'It's on *Melrose Place*. Haven't you ever seen *Melrose Place*? That's where some of them work on *Melrose Place*, at D & D Advertising.'

I say that, perhaps there are some similarities with the television show, but I am sure that the people I work with are much uglier.

He says: 'Have you ever done anything famous? Anything I would have heard of?'

I say no, not particularly.

He says: 'I once had a guy in the car who did those signs they put on the boots of Ford taxis that say *I'd rather be driving a Holden*.'

I ask him if the guy acted like he was proud of the signs.

He says: 'Sure. Wouldn't you be?'

DAY TEN

I have decided to start drinking at every opportunity. The nights I can get away from work on time I can go out with my co-workers and get drunk and vent my reptile aggressions, then catch a taxi home and drink some more in front of the television.

But tonight I work late. I leave my cubicle every fifteen minutes with a two-dollar coin in my hand, stomp down to the repurposed soft-drink machine, put the money in, and return with a can of beer. Before I leave for the night I distribute the great pile of empty cans I have made across the office, one in each rubbish bin. I am not so worried about looking like a drunk as I am worried that the boss will think I have been having fun.

Everything seems to be falling apart. I am filled with a great anger, directed at some amorphous and ill-defined cause. I feel like I have been swallowed by a giant protoplasm. Only the most mediocre of thoughts and impulses can resist the digestive properties of the protoplasm, only the blandest of substances remain after being systematically dumbed-down to the point where only an imbecile could find joy in its excretions. Everything is turning into cheese. I sway and stumble, faint with the overpowering stench of cheese. I rush out of the office, and as I collide with a chair on my way out it crumbles into pieces like an over-matured cheddar.

DAY ELEVEN

I work late again. My days are becoming foggy and incoherent. Only at night, after the boss has left, do my thoughts begin to clear. At six o'clock every evening the air-conditioning in the building automatically shuts off; by three in the morning the office is so hot I feel like a lone astronaut stranded on an alien desert planet without hope of rescue. I lean my forehead against the glass of the inside wall and stare down at the glass and steel garden on the ground floor. The view is the same, day or night, thanks to a series of spotlights positioned to overwhelm any natural light passing through the atrium's glass roof.

I am hot and I am drunk and I need a break. I take the elevator down and leave the building and cross the road to the twenty–four-hour supermarket.　　　　　I like supermarkets.

　　The air is cool inside the supermarket and Frank Sinatra is singing over the supermarket PA. There is only one checkout chick and one security guard in the place, and they watch me closely as I walk down the vacant aisles. I imagine they are my checkout chick and my security guard, and I am Richie Rich and everything in the store is mine. I feel happier than I have been at any time since I started working.

　　I pay close attention to every product I walk past; the package design and the printing quality of everything on the shelves. After I have walked down every aisle I make an off-hand purchase and reluctantly leave.

　　I stand outside the supermarket and look up at the building I work in. If I was going to write a story about my experiences I would call it 'The Office of Stupidity', after the story 'The House of Stupidity' by Alberto Savinio, the brother of the painter de Chirico. In the story 'The House of Stupidity' a telamon, an architectural support in the form of a human male figure, decides that the occupants of the house he holds up are too stupid to deserve his continued support. The telamon detaches himself from the building and the building collapses and kills the inhabitants. In the story I would write I would include a similar climax, but I am unsure how I could engineer such a collapse. A house is built on a human scale: the removal of a single figure can destroy a house. An office is a different matter. The removal of a single figure from an office has no effect at all, except that the remaining figures receive small pay rises to give them back a sense of security.

A military historian, attempting to write the history of a war of attrition, sifts through the records of the day-to-day events of the war and chooses to record those events which, although unremarkable at the time, can in retrospect be seen to have been the turning points in the battle. I use my security card to enter the building. I walk past the security guards and the closed shops in the foyer and use my security card to open the lift doors and then use the card to get the lift to go to my floor and again to open the door of the office. Each time I put the card in the slot the wrong way or I push a door that should be pulled or I pull a door that should be pushed. I start getting angry.

I get another beer and sit down at my cubicle in front of the computer. I still have to finish work on the tourism job. The last few days I have been touching up a map of the northern half of Australia and the southern part of the Asian continent, scanned from an atlas, and then marking the major air routes between the two. The biggest part of the job had been obscuring any distinguishing features on the original map. The boss wanted to use the money assigned for the map on an overseas trip for himself.

I have heard that maps and street directories sometimes have non-existent towns or streets or countries marked on them. This gives the legal owners of the maps an easy way to prove that their maps have been reproduced illegally. I had tried to check that there were no non-existent places on the map I was working on by comparing my map with maps from different atlases. I found nothing. At first I had planned to erase any non-existent places I discovered, but now I decided to leave them where they were. I feel envious of the people I imagine living in non-existent streets in non-existent towns and in non-existent countries. They have none of the hassles I have: no matter what they choose to do in the real world, they can always go home to a place where nobody can find them.

I zoom the window in on Japan. About a hundred kilometres off the coast I draw a small irregular shape, and in four-point type I label the shape *Monster Island*. Then I finish my beer and go home.

DAY TWELVE

I get to work early. The beggars are already out: they know that today is payday for most of the office workers. Most of the beggars are faking illnesses. I push my way past a man displaying a leg ulcer which looks like a cow spleen wrapped around his leg.

I forgot about the office party tonight. For a minute I think I am going crazy from lack of sleep. The whole office is full of plastic palm trees, plastic tropical fruit, surfboards and plastic bamboo, and the desks have all been covered with patterned barkcloths. 'Quiet Village' is playing over the PA system, and all of the staff are lined up outside of the darkroom, where one by one they are getting changed out of their street clothes and into either Hawaiian shirts or floral wraparound dresses. At least I am already dressed appropriately.

There is a Post-It note in the middle of the screen of my computer: the boss wants to see me. I feel a little sick at the sight of it. I drink a couple of cups of coffee, clean up my desk, twiddle my thumbs, then I go to the boss's office.

He smiles at me as I sit down. He says: 'I want to know if you can think of anyone I can get to help out *staff member X*. We have to think about these things. We have to know that the work will get done.

'What if *staff member X* got run over by a bus tomorrow? We have to think of these possibilities.'

I tell him there is nobody I can think of and I walk out before he can force the issue. I know what he really wants to know: he wants me to tell him if there is anyone I know who will do the job of *staff member X* for fifty cents less an hour than he currently pays *staff member X*. If I gave him a name, *staff member X* would be out of a job as soon as the boss can manage it, contract or no contract.

I am sick of this monkey business. I am sick of living on the Planet of the Apes.

At lunchtime everyone queues up outside the darkroom to change back into their street clothes, and they queue up again when they get back.

The transition from day to night is marked only by the point in time when it becomes acceptable for me to be drinking while I work. The office party is being held on the floor below me and from my cubicle I can hear the office band, the Pisspots, playing bad rock and roll music. I don't mind so much: I have almost finished the tourism job and nobody has spotted Monster Island. Instead of going to the red devil with my money I go downstairs to the party every fifteen minutes, where the beer is free.

The girl standing behind me in the beer queue taps me on the shoulder. She says: 'Didn't we go to university together?'

I tell her she looks familiar. I ask her what she is doing here.

She says: 'I'm in AE. What are you doing here?'

I have no idea what AE is. I say: 'Well, you know, I'm in the design department. I'm stuck here on a three-month contract.' I roll my eyes on the last sentence, and the pitch of my voice descends.

She says: 'Don't worry. I'm sure that if they are happy with your work you'll get a permanent position.'

I say: 'That's not what I meant.'

She says: 'I don't understand.'

She lets me take both her hands in mine and I bring them close to my face. I can see thick brown hairs protruding from the sleeves of her jacket and coarse stubble on the backs of her hands. I let go and then turn back to the queue.

Before I started doing this type of work I thought advertising was a cynical business. I thought that the people who worked in advertising would regard their work with a certain regret, with some embarrassment, or at least with a sense of humour. But I am the only cynic. I am the only one who thinks that corporate culture is something that grows in a Petri dish. I am the only one.

I take my beer and go back to my cubicle. I try to keep working but I am too upset to concentrate. Somewhere inside me is a great speech waiting to be born, full of fire and searing vision, that will burn itself into the minds of everyone in the building. After my speech, no-one will be able to look at what they are doing without thinking of my words.

I take a biro and write the letters C-H-E-E-Z on the knuckles of my right hand and the words S-L-A-C-K on the knuckles of my left. I return to the office party. When the band finishes their next song I stand up on stage and push over the singer. Then, doing my best Robert Mitchum impersonation, I say into the microphone:

'Little people, you are all looking at my fingers. Would you like me to tell you the little story of right hand/left hand? The story of CHEEZ and SLACK? C-H-E-E-Z! It is with this mouse hand we make the CHEEZ, we strike the blow that lays our souls low. S-L-A-C-K! You see these fingers, dear hearts? These idle fingers have veins that run straight to the soul, for without SLACK we are not alive, without SLACK we are just machines. The SLACK hand, friends, the hand of idle thoughts and possibilities. Now watch, and I'll show you the story of corporate advertising life. Those fingers, dear hearts, is always a-warring and a-tugging, one agin t'other. Now watch 'em! Old brother SLACK hand, SLACK hand he's a-fighting, but in this life there's too much CHEEZ and never enough SLACK. It looks like SLACK's a goner. He's being buried in CHEEZ! It's CHEEZ that's going to win, it's CHEEZ that always wins. What does that make us? Mice? And with so much CHEEZ, what kind of place is this? Let me ask you, brothers and sisters, are we living on the MOON?'

DAY FIFTEEN

The first day of the new week and my computer has started to play up. The screen has always been jittery, and I barely have enough memory in the thing to be able to work on it anyway. Now the hard drive is starting to stick. If I turn off the machine or reset it, it takes half an hour to get it started again. As the most recently hired employee I was given the oldest computer in the place, a real heritage item. The only chance I have of getting another computer is to wait until someone gets fired and then grab their machine before anyone else gets to it.

Until that happens I am going to have to live like a nomad, migrating from one cubicle to another, and using other people's computers when they are out.

I go into the boss's office. I say: 'My computer's not working.'

He says: 'It was working before.'

I say: 'I'm sure it was. It doesn't work now.'

He says: 'It was working before.' He turns the page of the brochure he is reading.

I say: 'Look, I need a new computer. I can't do any work until I get a new computer. The computer's no good.'

He says: 'It was working before.'

I say: 'The only way I will be able to get anything done is by using other people's computers when they've gone out.'

He says: 'No, you can't do that. You'll be stopping other people from getting their work done.'

I say: 'But my fucking computer isn't fucking working.'

He gets angry and says: 'It was working *before*.'

The boss has the biggest computer in the place, with four times more memory than any other machine and a huge chain of external hard drives. The boss never trashes anything on his computer. It is like a **software museum**. Every version of every software package ever made still lives on his hard drives: Adobe Illustrator 1.0, Illustrator 1.1, the ill-named Illustrator 88, Illustrator 3.0, Illustrator 3.2, Illustrator 4.0, Illustrator 5.0, Illustrator 5.5, as well as every letter of hiring and of dismissal he has ever written, every Mission Statement and Vision Statement and Business Statement he has ever started to write before getting bored and asking someone else to write it for him, and records of every sneaky trick he has every played on his underlings, written up and addressed to his superiors as efficiency drives and re-engineering plans. I know all this because he forgot to lock his office door one night and **one of the other designers** looked.

When he runs out of space on his computer he buys another hard drive and has someone add it to the chain. The boss would be more productive with an Etch-A-Sketch.

At lunchtime I go to a disposal store and buy one of those gun-shaped things people use to ignite gas stoves and barbecues. When everyone else has gone home for the night I open up the case of my computer and spark the fucker to death.

DAY SIXTEEN
I switch on my computer and a cloud of black smoke comes out. But do you think I get a new computer?

DAY SEVENTEEN
I have given up. The tourism job is finished. I have no computer and no assignments. Any big job I get in future I will have to palm off on someone else. All that I am leaving for myself is the occasional car ad. Lesson One: take the supplied photograph of the car driving along a winding road. Leave a white rectangle of space at the bottom. Put the words: 'The new *such-and-such*' at the top of the photograph, and put the word 'Only' and the price of the car at the bottom. Put the copy from the copy writer and the logo of the manufacturer in the white box. That's it. If that's all you have to do in a day then you have a fair amount of time left over to do some thinking for yourself.

I have a plan. Starting today, I will go into the boss's office every morning and annoy him by asking when I am going to get a new computer. I know that it is going to be cheaper to get rid of me than spend money on new equipment. I just wonder how long it will take the boss to work it out.

After I have annoyed the boss I am free for the rest of the day. I start to spend my time more productively. I have rediscovered the childhood pleasure of scratching my back by rubbing up against door frames. At lunchtime I go shopping.

I buy a new watch, a laser disc player with Karaoke Option in case I ever need it and the biggest couch I can find, which I have covered in a green cotton fabric. After lunch I watch videotapes of the English-dubbed Japanese television version of Wu Ch'êng-En's *Monkey* on the video-editing suite. I take a nap in my cubicle. I stomp around the office and roar. I stuff around.

I wait until the boss goes home for the night before I start doing any real work. The thing is, I have never thought of myself as being *in* advertising. I think of myself as a hired gun, employed by cattle barons to get rid of some pesky settlers. I don't have to like cows to be good at my job. But now I have started thinking about trying it out. The boss is always saying that we are in the business of communication. I have something I want to communicate myself.

I start by looking through the archive of finished adverts and campaigns. I find the cover image used on one of the boss's internally distributed Vision Statements. Someone had put together a montage of the disembodied heads of the executive officers of the company, my boss included, floating above the city like tie-wearing gods.

I deal with the city first. Most of the buildings are in the Victorian style, covered with ornamentation copied without reason or purpose from Classical times. I know that ornamentation is used in both architecture and advertising to conceal flaws: I am, after all, employed to conceal flaws.

But I also know that these ornaments once had meaning. As Savinio wrote:

The Greeks conceived of nothing, not even an architectural detail, that did not reflect a moral necessity. And those who still know how to decipher their temples and other buildings read them like parts of a Platonic dialogue.

I start to return the buildings to their original forms: the temples of the Greeks where human sacrifices were left to the gods. The columns become figures with slit throats, bound by cavetto mouldings that I turn into ropes. The flutings of the columns form blood vessels and hollow conduits of bone down which the blood of the sacrificed victims flows into the ground. Above and below the fascias of the buildings are rows of vertebrae and the triglyphs become droplets of fat and coagulated body fluids. The dentils become great rows of teeth, and the moulding on the architraves becomes rows of foetuses and the heads of my ancestors, their blood streaming down the cyma and leaving trails along the curved surface. The tympanum on the fronts of buildings become drums made from human skin, with the viscera of the victims laid out on the surface of the drums as if for a feast. The corbels on the corners of the buildings become elbows and ears, and in the shadows of the concave mouldings beneath the feet of the columns can be seen the tiny mote-like souls of the dead.

Above the city fly the executive officers like Japanese vampires, with bat's wings attached to either side of their heads and, instead of neckties, their own entrails hang down from their throats: I reveal them to the world as they truly are, as the parasitic rulers of a city built from sacrificed flesh.

DAY EIGHTEEN TO DAY TWENTY-ONE

I spend my next few days wasting time and my nights working on the Vision Statement. I am very tired but I no longer care. In the clothing shops on the ground floor of the building stand female mannequins dressed in the season's colours. They are the perfect employees, the ideal representatives of the human race in the physical world, incapable of boredom or resentment at the stupid poses they are forced to assume and subject to only the most minimal effects of wear and tear. Moulded without generative equipment, they come fitted with nipples to suckle factory-produced infants.

Once the Vision Statement is ready I begin **making colour prints on the office's Linotronic printer,** then I roll up the prints and hide them in an unused storage cupboard. I finish printing on Saturday, day twenty. I come back to the office on Sunday night, day twenty-one. I take the prints and begin sticking them on the inside windows of the office with double-sided tape, one print for each window. When I am finished the outside world is completely concealed for view. Then I sit in my cubicle and **wait** for morning.

DAY TWENTY-TWO

The twenty-second day of my incarceration is a special day. It is the first Monday of the new month, the day the boss has to submit his budget for the last month and his requirements for the next. So I know what is coming.

At around eight-thirty the first of my co-workers start shuffling into the office. Nobody makes a comment or even seems to notice anything is different: perhaps they think the new decoration is part of a strategy to increase productivity thought up by the boss. Stranger things have happened.

I have to wait until one in the afternoon before the boss calls me up and asks me in to his office.

He says: 'There isn't any work for you at the moment, so you can go home for the week.'

This isn't quite what I was expecting.

I say: 'You're not firing me?'

He says: 'No. Come back next week.'

I say: 'So, in other words, you've had me working here as a freelance designer on only a full-timer's wage? You fucking slimy little monkey, what about my contract?'

He says: 'What contract? You don't have a contract. Show me the contract. Go home.'

I really start to blow up. He keeps talking: 'I thought when we employed you that you were a creative person. Maybe I was wrong. You have to be creative in this business. All you've done is whine about your computer being broken. We don't want people who see *problems*. We want people who see *solutions*. Go home for now. I will call for you next week. Go home.'

I only have to lean against the building and the whole place collapses. Then I stomp on the other buildings around me. My spine has extended at the base to form a full-length tail, and I swing it around, demolishing the supermarket, then I bring it down on a Volvo-full of accountants. I have reverted to my true form.

When I get bored with stomping everything I realise I have no idea what I am going to do next. So I wait for the dust to settle. I want to make sure the boss hasn't made it out alive.

I lean down and look through the rubble. Then I start to think: I forgot to put in my last invoice, and my rent is due in a couple of weeks. I am going to have to think of something fast.

On the street I see the door girl from the nightclub waving to me. I pick her up and put her on my shoulder. I say: 'Where would you like to go?'

She says: 'Head towards the bay.'

At the deepest point the water only comes up to my waist. The weather is quite pleasant: I haven't been outside during daylight for at least a week.

I say: 'Where are we going exactly?'

She says: 'Monster Island, stupid.'

BRING ME THE HEAD OF DORA KENT

Dora Kent and her son, Saul Kent, lived in Riverside, California. They lived together until Dora contracted organic brain syndrome in 1984 and had to be moved to a nursing home.

Saul visited the nursing home every weekend. On each visit he would bring Dora three boxes of Kellogg's Pop Tarts and a copy of the latest *Weekly World News*. Every day for breakfast, Dora's nurse would remove the Mylar foil from the Pop Tarts and then heat them for thirty seconds in Dora's Taiwanese-built microwave.

Toasters had been banned at the nursing home since Betty Frule, from Room 262, left a Strawberry Pop Tart in her toaster for too long. Flames eighteen inches high sprouted from the toaster slots, as if from a dual-nozzle blowtorch, and set alight the polyester-blend kitchen curtains. In less than five minutes Betty Frule's kitchen was a gutted mess of blistered Formica. They moved Betty Frule across the hall to room 264: her relatives claimed that it was the shock that killed her three weeks later.

Saul still brought Pop Tarts to his mother, even though the microwave made the pastry go soggy and the heat-retaining, sugar-based fillings would sometimes burn her mouth and tongue. Saul kept a record of the Pop Tart deliveries in a small notebook. There were nine flavours: one week he would bring Strawberry, Milk Chocolate and Cherry, the next week he would bring Brown Sugar Cinnamon, Blueberry and Chocolate Fudge, and the week after he would bring Vanilla Creme, Raspberry and Grape. The next week the cycle would start again at the beginning. The system worked well. Then in 1991, Kellogg's began selling a new, additional flavour: Apple Cinnamon. This tenth flavour would have complicated Saul Kent's accounting procedure, but by 1991 Dora Kent was dead.

Dora Kent never left the United States. She had been bedridden for years with osteoporosis and atherosclerosis, and the organic brain syndrome she suffered from made her mind increasingly feeble. She had little to do during the day; she spent most of her time reading the *Weekly World News* and planning the world trip she would take if her illnesses miraculously abated. The *Weekly World News* provided her with interesting tourist locations. When she read a story she thought was particularly interesting she would mark the place where the story occurred in red pen on a map of the world she had found between the pages of an old *National Geographic*. In Australia she had marked Melbourne and Sydney. In Melbourne, she read, scientists had invented a lie-detector paper, which turned red when someone had just told a lie. In Sydney, a squad of deaf cheerleaders, posing for a publicity photograph, had been crushed by a train. They had formed a human pyramid on the railroad tracks when the photographer, who was using a telephoto lens, heard the train coming. He tried to alert the deaf girls to the danger, but the girls could not hear his screams. Then he ran toward them, waving his arms, but before he could reach them the train cut their bodies to pieces.

Saul Kent worked at the Alcor Life Extension Foundation. At Alcor, they freeze the recently dead so that at some unspecified time in the future, when medical technology has improved, the people can be brought back to life. As in any profession, cryonics researchers have developed an extensive, specialised language to describe their work, and to create a sense of community within the profession.

Dead people are said to have *deanimated*. If they are then frozen, a process which is called *suspension*, they are said to have been suspended, or placed in *biostasis*, or to be *potentially alive*. Informally, the frozen are referred to as *corpsicles*. If only the head is frozen, the process is called a *neurosuspension* or, informally, a *head job*. When they are brought back to life some time in the future, they will have been *reanimated*, and will enter their *second life-cycle*. Those who choose not to be frozen are said to be *Deathoids*, and to have inherited *Deathoid prejudices*.

The brain is a sensitive organ, and deteriorates rapidly after blood has stopped passing through it. The sooner a brain is frozen after death, the less damage the brain will suffer. Ideally, a patient would be suspended while still alive, to minimise damage to their brain from oxygen starvation. But there are legal complications: every possible attempt must be made to revive a dying patient, until the damage is so great that revival is considered impossible. There is no precise moment of death: the transition, in all but the most violent of situations, is gradual. The only certainty of death is that a patient is beyond any chance of reviving, and even then, as in Poe's 'The Premature Burial', mistakes are sometimes made.

Saul Kent and Dora Kent had both signed up for neurosuspensions. In December 1987, Dora Kent contracted pneumonia, and Saul had his mother moved out of the nursing home and on to the Alcor premises.

Shortly after midnight on Friday, December 11, 1987, the staff surgeon called up each member of the suspension team.

> He said: Hello Fred.
> Were you in bed?
> It's Dora Kent.
> I'm afraid she's dead.
> We're going to cut off her head.

Bring Me the Head of Dora Kent

He said: Hi John.
No, nothing's wrong,
Dora's gone.
We'll need you along.

He said: Hi Charles,
Sorry to call you after hours.
Hurry over, Dora's dead,
And would you mind bringing some flowers?

Dora Kent had a complicated death. Since she was already on the premises, the Alcor staff decided to begin the suspension process at once, rather than wait for a licensed physician to arrive to pronounce her dead and fill out the required paperwork. They attached Dora to a heart–lung resuscitator to keep the blood and oxygen circulating through her brain. Then they injected her body with a large dose of barbiturates to prevent the unlikely yet disturbing possibility that the resuscitator might resuscitate her.

Then the staff surgeon opened Dora's chest and connected her heart directly to a perfusion pump. Then they immersed her body in a bath full of ice-water. A heat exchanger kept the water at near freezing, and the perfusion pump was turned on, to replace her blood with a glycerol solution. Once she had sufficiently cooled and her body was filled with glycerol, they prepared to remove her head.

An electric Desoutter saw works on a different principle than the usual handyman's electric saw. Instead of rotating, the blade of a Desoutter saw oscillates back and forth. The blade itself is shaped like a slice of cake, with teeth on the rounded, cutting edge. The advantage of using a reciprocating Desoutter saw over a rotating blade is simple: a rotating blade will throw **bone, blood and tissue fragments** over a considerable distance, which is both unpleasant and unhygienic.

When they were finished, they wrapped her head in a protective foil shroud and took it to the cephalarium vault in the basement of the building. There they put her head inside a stainless-steel capsule filled with liquid nitrogen and placed it on a shelf between a capsule containing the frozen head of a television repairman and the frozen head of a moderately successful real estate agent.

Saul Kent had contracted the Buena Park Chapel and Mortuary to cremate Dora's discarded body. To get a cremation permit, the mortuary needed a death certificate, which Saul did not have. So the officials at the Buena Park Chapel and Mortuary tried to get a cremation permit from the public health service. The public health service refused, since no physician had been in attendance at Dora Kent's death, and given the peculiar state of Dora Kent's body. A few days later, some officers from the county coroner's office went to Alcor and took away Dora's discarded remains.

Adventure Golf, Pigeon Forge, TN, USA.
Birthplace of Dolly Parton.

An autopsy was performed, and the deputy coroner signed a death certificate stating that the cause of death had been pneumonia, listing atherosclerosis and organic brain syndrome as contributing factors. On December 23, Dora Kent was cremated.

The next day, Christmas Eve, an NBC camera crew knocked on the front door of Saul Kent's home. When Saul Kent appeared, an NBC reporter asked Saul what he thought of the story in today's paper.

Saul said: What story is this?

The reporter said:
Look here and here!
On page four and page five.

You cut off your Mom's head,
Or so they have said,
while she was still very much alive.

And now the police have charged you
With homicide.

Raymond Carillio, the county coroner, had already made quite a name for himself. He had performed an autopsy on Liberace earlier in the year. Liberace had been embalmed and was about to be interred at the famous Forest Lawn Cemetery, when Carillio demanded that an autopsy had to be conducted.

Autopsy, autopsy,
Poor Liberace.
Loved by the many
His baroque personality
Irritated the few.

His personal preference,
In sex and his dress sense,
Made him a target
For unjust injustice.

But this indignity
Did not cheapen his dignity
With the blue-rinse set
Who had paid his rent.

His classical flourishes
And humorous anecdotes
If not for the high brow
Endeared him to millions.

His unfortunate death
Was needlessly paraded
Before the jaded.

Raymond Carillio announced the findings of the autopsy to the press from the front steps of the Riverside County administrative building.

He cleared his throat and then said:
As you know, Liberace is dead.
His agent has said
That the reason he's dead
Was heart failure caused
By subacute encephalopathy.

With this conclusion I must
Say that I,
And my staff,
Were unhappy.

I had tissue samples taken,
As is regulation.
And I discovered that the true cause of death,
And I do not wish to create a furore,
Was the Acquired Immune Deficiency disorder.

When Raymond Carillio read the findings of and circumstances surrounding Dora Kent's autopsy, he decided to begin a further investigation. The presence of barbiturates in Dora Kent's body led Raymond Carillio to suspect foul play. He alerted the press and the police, in that order, and held a press conference. Raymond Carillio announced that he was going to hold a criminal investigation into the Dora Kent case. Since her body had already been cremated, he would have to perform an autopsy on Dora Kent's head.

Two weeks later, the Riverside police raided the Alcor Foundation for evidence, but Dora Kent's head was

Liberace Museum, Las Vegas, NV, USA.

no longer there. The Riverside police chief phoned Raymond Carillio and told him they had not found Dora Kent's head. Carillio told the police chief:

> Bring me the head of Dora Kent.
> I want to know where it is and where it went.
> If you don't find it,
> It's your head instead.
> You got that?
> Well good,
> Now do what I said.

On Christmas morning, Saul Kent drove to the Alcor Foundation. He packed three tanks of liquid nitrogen in the trunk of his Honda Civic, then he put the stainless-steel capsule containing Dora Kent's head on the front passenger seat.

Saul Kent drove off. He turned on the car radio. Frank Sinatra was singing 'All of Me'. Saul Kent began to cry. As he drove he looked sideways at the stainless-steel capsule. He began to talk. He said: Don't worry, Mom. Everything will be okay. The future will be a wonderful place. There will be no wars and no poverty and everyone will live forever. Everything will be clean, and we will be able to travel around the world at the speed of light, and go for holidays on different planets. People will live on floating islands, and robots will do all the housework. Computers will run the planet, and everyone will live a life of leisure. You can be young again, in a new, genetically engineered body that you can design yourself. Or you can have a robot body, with as many arms and legs as you want. The future will be just like Heaven. The future will be just like Heaven on Earth.

Saul Kent drove around California for the next ten days. He told his mother they should keep to the backroads: the police would be looking for them. He kept the radio on, waiting to hear the news reports about a fugitive from the law, a murderer who had cut off and stolen his own mother's head. He debated whether they should try to make it to Mexico, but he was sure that the police would have set up roadblocks. He had to find some place where his mother would be safe.

Every few hours, he would stop the car at a deserted tourist attraction and top up the capsule with liquid nitrogen. He parked next to the Ronald Reagan Memorial Tree in Arcata, the World's Largest Olive in Lindsay, and the Richard Nixon Birthplace and Library in Yorba Linda. He stopped beneath the shadow of a forty-foot tall statue of a topless Amazon aiming a bow and arrow at the sky in the parking lot of a dental practice in Auburn, and stopped next to a twenty-one-foot tall pyramid in Felicity that contained a circular plaque claiming to mark the centre of the world.

The first liquid nitrogen tank ran out at the World's Largest Artichoke in Castroville. Saul Kent drove on, past

Fairyland, the Hug-A-Pig Pet Farm, Chuck E. Cheese University, the Haunted Toys-R-Us, the Church Made of Straw and the Birthplace of Kool-Aid. He spent one night at the Lawrence Welk Resort Village in Escondido, another night in the Caveman Room of the Madonna Inn in San Luis Obispo, and another night in a rail car at the Caboose Motel in Dunsmuir.

The second tank of liquid nitrogen ran out at the Wigwam Village in Rialto. Saul Kent was afraid to buy any more liquid nitrogen, in case the police traced the purchase. He stared at some of Gandhi's ashes, housed in the Self-Realisation Fellowship's Lake Shrine in Pacific Palisades, and waited for some idea to come to him. After two hours, he returned to the car and started to drive toward Anaheim, smiling at the billboards that counted down the miles to Disneyland.

Saul Kent registered under a false name at the Disneyland Hotel. He left Dora's head in the hotel room while he shopped on Main Street USA. He bought a two-wheeled luggage trolley and a vinyl Mickey Mouse carry-bag with a shoulder strap, then went back to the hotel room.

Saul spent the afternoon in Tomorrowland, riding the roller-coaster on Space Mountain. That night he left the hotel with the stainless-steel capsule on the trolley and the carry-bag over his shoulder. He was wearing a yellow boiler

Niagara Falls Motel, Niagara Falls, NY, USA.

suit with the Alcor logo stitched on the breast pocket. He walked down Main Street USA, past the railroad station, the Walt Disney Story exhibit, the Diamond Horseshoe Jamboree reservation office and reached City Hall, where three security guards, dressed as Huey, Dewey and Louie, stopped him.

Saul said: I'm here to do a maintenance check. I know I'm early this month, but I was a little worried about the last test results. The evaporation rate was a little high, so to be safe I came back early.

Huey nodded to Saul, then the three characters went back inside City Hall. Saul kept walking down Main Street until he reached the end, and then walked through Fantasyland until he got to Cinderella's Castle. He went to a service door beside the main entrance of the castle, hidden behind some bushes, took a key from his pocket and unlocked it. Inside the door, a short neon-lit corridor led to an elevator. Saul took the elevator to the top floor.

The elevator opened on to a large apartment, furnished in the style of a turn-of-the-century middle-class American home. A large wooden chest stood in the middle of the room, just large enough to hold a human body. Saul parked the luggage trolley next to the chest and put down the carry-bag.

He took a pair of heavy, insulated gloves out of the carry-bag and put them on. He took another key from his pocket and unlocked the chest. The chest, lined with stainless steel and several layers of insulation, contained the frozen body of Walt Disney in a bath of liquid nitrogen.

Saul took a large poker from the stand next to the fireplace. He used the poker to lever Walt Disney's head and upper torso out of the liquid nitrogen. Then he unwrapped the foil from around Walt Disney's head and neck.

Saul took a Desoutter saw out of the carry bag and plugged it into a concealed power socket near the base of one wall. His face was flushed and his hands started to shake. Saul said: I'm sorry.

> Walter Elias Disney
> Frozen in perpetuity
> His dreams of immortality
> Have now become unlikely.

> The shaking hands!
> The shaking blade!
> The cuts are made
> The switch is made.

> What else could Saul do?
> There wasn't the room
> In the capsule for two.

JACKIE CHAN

On a good day I get up early and write until lunchtime. Then I call up a friend and we go out for lunch, either somewhere nearby or in the city centre. After we eat we usually wander around and do some shopping. I might pick up a book or a CD or a toy of some kind. Then I go home and work; not writing, but the kind of work I do to make a living. At night I watch television.

That is what I do on a good day, but most days never go that well. Most days something else comes up: I have errands to run, or I am feeling too lazy or too tired to write and I stuff around instead, or I have a job to do for a client with a deadline that precludes any other activity.

Work and the city are my two main distractions. I have no regular daily routine. My clients treat me as if I am available twenty-four hours a day; I never know when I am going to have to work, or where, or for how long. I am not very good at saying no to a client, and I can always spend their money, but the lack of a daily routine makes it difficult for me to eat regular meals, let alone concentrate on writing.

Then there is the city. I like to wander about. At any particular time I can easily come up with a dozen reasons for going into the city. When I am out my clients cannot contact me. Time in the city is stolen time, the only free time I have, and the only opportunity I have to get some exercise.

Since I moved to Melbourne about ten years ago I have left its boundaries less than a dozen times. I have only been overseas once, when I was a kid. I am not sure how old I was but I could work it out if I had to. I was born in 1970, and I was in New Zealand when the space shuttle *Challenger* exploded. In fact I was in the shower in a hotel bathroom when my father yelled the news to me from outside the bathroom door. This event is all that I really remember about New Zealand, the thoughts and sensations I experienced while I stood in a hotel shower and my father told me the space shuttle had just exploded. I could probably draw a floor plan of the hotel bathroom.

Since I moved to Melbourne I have been happy to limit my travels to places I can reach by tram or other public transport and a couple of weekend trips to the country in someone else's car.

I refuse to believe that I will learn anything by travelling overseas. Most of my friends have travelled and, if anything, the effects have been detrimental. Still, I am planning to go to Hong Kong before the Chinese take-over in 1997. I can justify myself: the book is almost finished and I need a holiday, somewhere my clients cannot reach me. I have a place I can stay in Hong Kong for free, and it would be a pity to miss out on an opportunity to visit Hong Kong before China takes control. I do not doubt that I will enjoy the trip. After all, I expect to do much the same things in Hong Kong as I do in Melbourne: eat out and wander around the shopping districts. As far as I am concerned, I will treat Hong Kong as a part of Melbourne that I am visiting for the first time and nothing more.

On a day in late March or early April 1996 I went out for lunch with a friend. I cannot remember if this was a good day or just an ordinary day: I might have been working on 'Powerhouse' that morning, or I might have got bored with some job I was doing from home for a client.

While we were looking for somewhere to eat we came across a disturbance: a film crew had blocked off the footpath for the length of three shop fronts. One of the shops was a bookshop. We stopped while I decided if I wanted to try and squeeze past the film crew to go inside. The footpath was covered with cables and the members of the film crew, all dressed in identical yellow parkas, were moving lights around the corner to where the actual shooting was taking place.

More than anything else, the scene reminded me of an intrusive surgical procedure. We kept walking, past the bookshop and the cables and the side street. One day I would like to edit an anthology of stories about cities described as bodies and bodies described as cities.

The idea first came to me when I was reading a nineteenth-century history of surgery that I had borrowed from a medical library. The book was structured as a chronological list, further divided by country. In the section describing the achievements of French surgeons I found an entry for a certain Nicholas de Blegny. The entry said that Nicholas de Blegny founded the first medical journal and, as an aside, mentioned that he also created the first street directory.

I have often thought about Nicholas de Blegny, a man I know nothing more about than what I have mentioned here, and the logic behind a surgeon devising the first street directory. I like to imagine Nicholas de Blegny as a pivotal historic figure, linking the vocabulary of surgery and anatomy with the vocabulary of architecture and urban planning. Many of the features of the modern city and architecture are described using terms borrowed from the language of anatomy:

    arterial roads,
    the circulation of people and of traffic,
    the heart of the city,
    the wings and arms of a building,
    the tail of a windmill,
    the throat of a chimney,
    the mouth of a side street where it enters a main road,
    footwalls,
    footpaths,
    the foot of the stairs,
    the knuckles of a hinge,
    the head of a bridge.

Shot tower, Melbourne Central.

A road that radiates from an intersection is called a leg;

bricks or stones placed at the top of a wall to prevent people from climbing over are called teeth;

the openings at the top of a cupola are called eyes;

wetlands and parks are called the lungs of a city;

a service building, anything from a garden shed to a train depot, is called a headhouse;

and when a building is gutted all that remains is a skeleton.

Surgeons in turn borrow from the language of architecture and urban planning:

the arches of the feet,

the bridge of the nose,

the column of vertebrae,

the atrium of the heart,

the canals of the circulatory system;

surgeons perform bypasses

and a blind pouch – a type of congenital vessel anomaly –

is called a cul-de-sac.

I chose not to watch the film crew as we walked past. I felt no curiosity about what they were filming: I imagined a more or less generic Australian film, either about middle-aged, middle-class people relating to each other in a fashionable inner suburb or a film about drug-addled middle-class kids failing to relate to each other in the same locations.

That night I got a phone call from another friend. He had also seen the film crew, but he had stopped to watch as Jackie Chan had a car door slammed into his head **five or six times,** in the same number of takes. My friend told me that Jackie Chan had just started shooting his new film in Melbourne, although it was going to be set in New York. Filming in Australia was cheaper than filming in America, and some of the streets around where I lived had been chosen as shooting locations for their resemblance to the streets of New York.

My friend had his own Jackie Chan story. He told it to me one day over lunch. Later I made him tell me the story again into a tape recorder, while we sat in an ice-cream shop. My friend had a sorbet of some kind; I probably had a double cone with caramel macadamia and, I think, banana-flavoured ice-cream.

My friend, like most of my friends, was trained as an architect, and he was on a working holiday in Kuala Lumpur when he met Jackie Chan:

'The Jackie Chan Kuala Lumpur story. Basically, Jackie Chan was in this huge mall called Lot Ten in Kuala Lumpur and there was a huge crowd. I didn't know he was going to be there, but I got there and there was a huge crowd and a buzz. I think there were heaps of posters and, I didn't even know about this, but he was there for some charity. There was a photographic exhibition on display in the mall and the photographs were also in this book you had to buy. Anyway, you could get autographs. Jackie arrived with huge amounts of security, and his sidekick Willie, who goes with him everywhere. So I went up on to the first level to look down. It was in this huge atrium. He's just this really small guy, but he's so stocky and unbelievably well-built, and he has just the largest face that you've ever seen. It's just huge.

'So anyway, I thought well, this is my chance. Being a fan, I was going to get his autograph.   How much of this is going in?'

I told him I hadn't made up my mind.

'Being a huge fan I thought I'm going to go get his autograph. But to get his autograph I had to buy the ten-ringgit Jackie Chan book. Well, there was the ten-ringgit and the twenty-ringgit book. The books were basically the same, photos from this exhibition put in this book, and the ten-ringgit had only a few less photos than the twenty-ringgit, so . . . I was with my friend and . . . anyway,   I thought I'd buy the cheap one.'

I asked how much a ringgit was worth.

'Ten ringgit is about five bucks and twenty ringgit is ten bucks. Honestly, the twenty-ringgit book wasn't better value, photograph by photograph.

'So I stood in this line. I honestly thought I wouldn't get through. I was the tallest person there. The queue was long, but not as long as I thought it was going to be. There were a lot of people hanging around, but not many people in the queue. So I thought this was pretty fun, this was going to be great, but I wasn't taking it too seriously.

'I was the next person to go up on to this little platform and everyone could see me and, I tell you, I got horribly nervous, terribly nervous. I didn't think I would . . . I thought it was so matter-of-fact, I didn't think I was going to get this nervous.

Dennis Daniel with Jackie Chan's autograph.

'I got nervous. I was next. I go up there, get on the stage. He's there, he sort of smiles – nice guy, very nice guy. And we sort of shake hands. It was a firm shake, so firm he crushed my hand. He sort of asked me how I'm going in English, but it was sort of broken. Apparently he knows a little English but he can't read or write it.

'So basically he asked me how I was going, and all of a sudden I found it very difficult to come up with any English words. I wanted to revert back to my mother tongue. The only thing I could think of to say was 'Cool, man'. But there was a bit of a gap between the cool and the man. So it came out as *cool . . . man*. To Jackie's credit he was still smiling but the security behind him were going really haywire: *Oh my God, we've got a live one here*. The snipers all of a sudden pointed to me.

'He sort of looked and smiled. I don't think he understood, but I think he knew there was some problem.

'Anyway, I got off the stage. My head went straight into the palms of my hands. I did that sort of John Cleese *Fawlty Towers* thing where he curls up on the ground. Jackie had signed the book, but he'd actually signed it on the wrong page. He'd signed it on a page where there was a photo of him sniffing the daisies, but I wanted him to sign on the page where he was in a kung fu stance.

'Anyway, my friend was there. This was a bit of a dangerous move, because it was one autograph per book, per person. But I gave her the book and said: "You've got to get the autograph on this page." I was in no danger at that point, but she was in a lot of danger because security was quite tight; you had to have paid for one of these books, because it was for charity. She wasn't as nervous as I was – she didn't really know whose hand she was shaking. This guy's a legend, he's got a steel plate in his head . . . and she got the autograph. So I've got a ten-ringgit book with two signatures and I tell you, both signatures are exactly the same. I think he's had a bit of practice writing it.

'So that's the Jackie Chan Kuala Lumpur story.'

My friend loaned me the ten-ringgit twice-autographed Jackie Chan book. The introduction to the book was in both Cantonese and English and said that the profits were going to be used to buy kidney machines for patients at the MAA-Medicare Dialysis Centre. The photographs, taken by the Japanese photographer Sumio Uchiyama over a period of fifteen years, showed Jackie in different locations, outfits and poses around the world:

Jackie Chan in an off-white fabric suit and tie,

Jackie Chan in knee-high pants and long socks,

Jackie Chan in a pink windbreaker crouching next to a little Anglo girl while they feed pieces of bread to two baby kangaroos,

Jackie on a porch cradling a kitten,

Jackie Chan in lederhosen outside a stucco-painted church,

Jackie Chan in South America wearing a coloured poncho and a three-cornered hat,

Jackie working out on a Nautilus machine,

Jackie taking a shower,

Jackie in bed,

Jackie in a European forest,

Jackie wearing beige multi-pocketed overalls and standing on the rim of a fountain in Mexico,

Jackie in formal wear leaning on a bicycle on a beach,

> Jackie in a tracksuit on a BMX bicycle,
> Jackie Chan and Samo Hung wearing tracksuits and standing in a kung fu pose inside a Gaudi cathedral.

Jackie Chan wasn't smiling in all of the photographs: in some of them he looked thoughtful, and sometimes melancholy, but in most of the photographs he was smiling. Between the photographs were inspirational messages, like: 'Exercise keeps our bodies fit, our minds alert and helps us stay away from DRUGS', and 'Don't walk in front of me / I may not follow / Don't walk behind me / I may not lead / Just walk beside me / And be my friend.'

By the next morning I had decided that I wanted to meet Jackie Chan. I called up some friends to see if any of them wanted to come with me to the film shoot. I was too scared to approach Jackie Chan on my own. I started to rehearse in my mind the things I would say and do when I met Jackie Chan, but the only solid idea I had was to smile at Jackie Chan with the biggest grin I could manage.

Everyone I called up was either out or too busy to come with me. I could have gone on my own, but instead I stayed home and, when I next walked down the street where they had been filming, the crew had moved on to another location. There was nothing I particularly wanted to ask Jackie Chan, and I had not really thought how I was going to bring about our meeting. Maybe I could try to get him aside and tell him that I was a writer and that I wanted to interview him.

The rest I had planned out. We would agree to meet at a restaurant, where I could bring along some friends. I would mostly be quiet and smile as much as I could while my friends did all the talking and I recorded the conversations on audio tape. Afterwards, like a good host, I would insist on paying for Jackie Chan's meal.

Although I had no questions, there were a few things I wanted to say to Jackie Chan. I wanted to tell Jackie Chan that I was very interested in the process he was going through of making a film in Melbourne which would be set in New York. I wanted to tell him that much of my own work involved the imposition of incongruous scenes upon real physical locations, although I tried to make the process explicit while he chose to conceal it. But mostly I wanted to emphasise the similarities between us. I wanted Jackie Chan to think I was interesting. I wanted Jackie Chan to like me. I wanted Jackie Chan to be my friend.

Over the next few weeks I saw Jackie Chan interviewed on a number of different television shows, and my friends would call to tell me where and when they had seen Jackie Chan filming. But I knew I would never have the courage to talk to Jackie Chan.

The whole time, I kept doing what I usually do: I wrote a little and I worked when clients asked me to. I had tried to force myself to write a certain number of words every day, preferably good words, but with work and other disruptions I was failing to keep up.

My editor has told me that a first novel by an Australian author can expect to sell from three to four thousand copies and a collection of short stories to sell half of that amount. If I am optimistic I can expect to sell two thousand copies of this book. On the one hand, an audience of two thousand people hardly justifies the time and effort of writing a book in the first place. On the other hand, two thousand people is a lot of people, more people than I expect to meet or would want to meet in my lifetime.

Of these two thousand anonymous people, I cannot imagine what a single one of them is like, or what we would have in common to talk about, or even if I would like them.

They say it is important to write with an audience in mind. Ideally, they would all be exactly the same as me. As an alternative, I can imagine these two thousand people as a **single mass.** I imagine the members of my audience as fairly average people, and as such I can impose standard characteristics on them. In an appendix to the reference work 'Metric Tables of Composition of Australian Foods' I found a description of the reference models used by food scientists to represent an average Australian woman and an average Australian man. Reference Woman is twenty-five years old and weighs fifty-eight kilograms. Reference Man is also twenty-five years old and weighs seventy-one kilograms.

I have no way of knowing if this book will be read by more members of one sex than another, so I will assume an even distribution of one thousand women and one thousand men. Using these figures, I can estimate an audience that weighs almost a hundred and thirty metric tonnes, as heavy as any dinosaur that ever lived.

When I write I try to keep in mind the expectation and desires of this large animal. I make certain concessions. I try to keep it entertained. I am even afraid of this animal and what will happen if it is disappointed with my efforts or feels little sympathy for me. Jackie Chan's audience is at least ten thousand times larger than my audience would ever be, an audience of more than two billion people. I am unable to imagine a creature of that size, or the sight that ten thousand creatures of the size of my own audience would make while standing on some vast plain.

I can only imagine Jackie Chan's audience by reducing it in scale to the size of a human being and its components to the size of individual cells. From this perspective I can see that Jackie Chan will never be my friend, any more than I would regard a single flake of skin with any particular affection.

I had not eaten breakfast and it was already lunchtime and one of my clients had called to say they had a job for me. I caught the usual tram to the city and then walked along Swanston Street to the Melbourne Central shopping centre.

Melbourne Central, the brochure says, is 'the throbbing, thriving heart of the world's most livable city'. I go there a lot, maybe three or four times a week, to buy Japanese confectionery from the Daimaru food court and to eat Japanese food at the Kujaku bistro on the ground floor, separated from the atrium proper by a glass wall. Melbourne Central covers most of two city blocks. It was designed by the Japanese architect Dr Kisho Kurokawa and cost the developer Kumagai Gumi more than a billion dollars. This is all in the brochure.

The circular atrium is ringed with balconies, like an amphitheatre, and is topped by a giant glass cone. In the centre of the atrium stands Coop's shot tower, built a hundred years ago for the manufacture of lead shot, but the rest of the atrium is filled with a bizarre Japanese version of Australian-style kitsch. A miniature hot-air balloon and a sixty-five per cent scale replica of the Wright brothers' biplane, both occupied by mannequins in period costume and suspended by cables from the conical atrium roof, circle the shot tower at irregular intervals. A twelve-metre-square television attached to one of the balconies displays the in-house television programming, and further along the wall is a giant, two-tonne Seiko fob-watch with a fob chain about twelve metres long. Every hour the fob-watch plays a sweeping, synthesised New Age version of 'Waltzing Matilda' and disgorges a mechanical marionette display: cockatoos, galahs and two cherubs move in time with the music. At the back of the watch is a transparent panel

The world's largest imitation Seiko fob-watch,
Melbourne Central.

through which koalas can be seen, living among the gears and cogs.

The rest of Melbourne Central is generic shopping mall. From the outside the entrances are large and easy to find, but from the inside the exits are hidden as much as is politely possible. The two main department stores, the Australian store Myer on the next block and the Japanese Daimaru, are connected by an above-street covered walkway, but the two stores are situated at the greatest distance from each other so that the usual shopper, going from one store to the other, will have passed the maximum amount of shop frontage in between.

From where I usually sit, in the Kujaku bistro on the ground floor, I cannot see the display but I am happy just to watch the tourists as, on the hour, they form a large mass in front of the shot tower and take photographs of the giant fob-watch as it disgorges. After I have eaten I wander around for a while and do some shopping.

That day I only wandered a little: I bought a packet of grape-flavoured, Pop Rock-encrusted candy floss and a book about the history of the zipper. As I left Melbourne Central I saw the tram I wanted to catch just leaving. I walked along Swanston Street and waited at the corner of Bourke Street for the next tram. The trams seemed to have stopped: no tram could be seen travelling toward me from either direction. I could see a number of trams, banked up and immobile on the far side of Princess Bridge, and just the next block down from me, on Collins Street, I could see two policemen had started redirecting the traffic. I had been in this situation before. Swanston Street would be blocked off for twenty minutes or so to allow a government car, carrying a foreign politician or a celebrity of some kind, or, for all I knew, an old school friend of the Premier that he wanted to impress, to drive along Swanston Street and up Bourke Street to Parliament House without interruption.

After twenty minutes with no trams the street corners got crowded with people waiting for the trams to start up again. I wondered if the visiting dignitaries would think that all these people were standing around just to catch sight of them as they drive past. I waited another ten minutes, then I walked down to Collins Street and went up to one of the policemen.

I said: 'What's the hold-up? How long am I going to be stuck here?' For a policeman he was very short.

He told me Jackie Chan was shooting a stunt: Jackie Chan was going to jump off the Princess Bridge. The policeman said he had no idea how long it was going to take. He said: 'Why don't you catch a taxi?'

So I caught a taxi. When I got to my client's office they told me they had just taken on a large contract with a three-week deadline and they wanted me to start work immediately. I said okay.

The Japanese have a word, *karoshi*, for death from overwork. The deadline was so tight, there was so much to do, and the client, my client's client, was so inflexible that I was working sixteen to twenty hours each day, and would probably have to work those kind of hours for the entire three-week period. The situation was extreme but not unusual. Like the cerebral equivalent of a long-distance runner, I have learned a few tricks to keep myself going. Don't stop working: if you stop for anything longer than a toilet break you will realise how tired you are. Don't eat: eating makes you sleepy. Drink sugary coffee and keep a large supply of sweets on hand; with luck, the office will be near a twenty-four-hour convenience shop or, even better, a twenty-four-hour supermarket. Alcohol also works as a stimulant, but only for as long as you keep drinking. And if you get a sharp pain in your side and your breath smells like acetone you have probably pushed yourself into the early stages of hypoglycaemia: ask if you can go home and sleep for a couple of days. That's a joke.

Most of the time, being a freelance worker means being treated like a very expensive roll of toilet paper. After a week you get sick, and you start to think about how many days of unpaid recovery time you are going to need when the job is finished. You start to worry about your health, any permanent damage you might be doing to yourself. The funny sick thing is, if you tell clients about your concerns they will just say: 'Oh.'

They don't care. When the job is finished they are going to flush you anyway. If they came into the office one morning and found you lying there, dead on the floor next to the computer, the first thing that would go through their minds is: 'He did *finish* the job, didn't he?'

You reach rock bottom when you get home at four o'clock on a Monday morning and you are so hungry you

The 'Paris End' of Collins Street, Melbourne.

go through your collection of restaurant flyers three or four times, hoping that this time, by some miracle, you will find a restaurant that does home delivery at four o'clock on a Monday morning. Then you give up and go to bed hungry, too tired to sleep and thinking about the new working week only four hours away.

I started catching taxis to and from work. Catching taxis involved less thinking. Jackie Chan continued filming around the city. I would make the taxi driver take a route that passed by the film crew every morning. I was yet to see Jackie Chan in the flesh: all that I could see as we drove past was a large crowd of onlookers and the occasional crew member wearing a bright yellow parka with the name of the film, *A Nice Guy*, printed on the back beneath a smiley logo.

Working those sorts of hours, you get burned out and your thoughts start to turn against you. The days and nights take on the qualities of an endless, boring dream, and when you do sleep you dream that you are still at work. I had a lot to do but very little to think about, except Jackie Chan and the book that I was never going to finish. **The biggest film star in Asia,** Jackie Chan had been trying to break into the American film market on and off for years, with little success until the release of *Rumble in the Bronx*, which was filmed in Vancouver. The majority of Americans will not watch a film unless it is set in America or the stars are Americans. So it made a lot of sense, monetary sense, for Jackie Chan to set this new film, shot in Melbourne, in New York.

And no-one was sure what would happen to the Hong Kong film industry after China started to govern Hong Kong. Both of Jackie Chan's parents lived in Australia, and I had heard that Jackie Chan held an Australian passport. He would be able to leave Hong Kong if he had to.

The book was on hold: I would have no time to write until I finished the job, which meant that I was going to miss the deadline in my contract. Every day I worked was another day the book was going to be late, in addition to the week in bed I was going to need to start feeling human again. And the way I was going, there was always the possibility that I was going to get a brain embolism and die before I got to write another word.

I finally had some questions that I wanted to ask Jackie Chan, questions that only I could ask. The questions related to my own situation. The questions were questions I had started to ask myself.

For the first time I began to think that my life would be easier if I lived in another city in another country. The feeling started when I first saw Jackie Chan filming in the city: the cables, the blockages caused by the crowds watching the film crew from the footpaths and haemorrhaging on to the street and the familiar places which I began to see as foreign, as if I was looking through Jackie Chan's eyes.

I had always believed that I would not be able to write if I lived in another city. I imagined that if I wandered the streets of Paris or New York or Rome or Berlin, all that I would be conscious of would be **the weight** of all the stupid clichés I had picked up about these cities, **the weight** of everything that had ever been written or said about them, pressing down on me like a great block of stone. There would be nothing that I could imagine that would relieve me from this pressure. At best I could try to write about the place I had left, the memories of a place I had sealed away as if I had mounted it in a snowdome, but no matter how hard I shook it up the place would remain dead to me.

A friend once suggested to me that there were only two types of people who travelled: tourists and refugees. I had started to feel like a refugee. This was how I saw it: the city was a different type of place when viewed by the driver of a moving car. There was a certain type of person, probably in the majority of people, who drove from one place to another without giving a thought to the city they were passing through. They were concentrating on getting to where they wanted to go. The faster the trip went, and the less distractions they experienced, the better.

Now, take the more extreme example of a person who lived in one of the better suburbs, in the kind of house preferred by the rich, with **a high, solid wall** facing the street to prevent anyone outside from looking in and anyone inside from having to look out. They could drive from their house to the car-park of the office they worked in or to the car-park of the more exclusive shopping centres. They would never need to go out on the street and they would never want to, for fear of having to deal with someone less well-off than they were. A person like that did not care about the city because they hardly knew it existed. When people like that are put in charge of the city they build a casino and lots of new freeways and overpasses and underpasses and lots of buildings that are just big sheds with angled façades and underground parking and offset the costs by cutting the funding to the public transport system.

Perhaps Melbourne was one of the last places where someone could still see the city as something more than just an obstacle for movement. Every day I travelled along fixed routes, not on a subway or on a train route walled off from the surroundings, but on a tram that ran along the middle of the street. I saw the city without distraction, without concern for the other traffic or for where I was going. I could look at the city with the eyes of a film-maker scouting for locations which, in a way, I was. The buildings and the people I saw, day after day, were almost as familiar as the objects which filled my own house. I saw every change that occurred in the city with the sharpened awareness of an *habitué*. And for a while I had noticed that things were changing for the worse.

I got a friend to help me finish the job I was working on. There was too much work for me to make the deadline without some help, and being stuck in the office on my own, night after night, was pretty lonely.

We were working on average twenty hours a day, every day. The job itself kept changing: as usual, the clients, my client's clients, kept changing their minds about what they wanted but refused to change the deadline accordingly. We spent a week working like that, and by the end we were both looking pretty hairy.

Saturday afternoon came around and I had an idea. I had *Son of Godzilla* playing in the office, on the video-editing suite, and we had stopped work to watch an action scene. I said: 'I am going to buy an electric shaver, a cordless shaver. It's the only way I am ever going to get time to shave.' We both got excited. By then, any excuse to get out of the office was a good excuse. We took my friend's car to the city and left it in the Melbourne Central underground car-park.

We ate at the Kujaku bistro, we watched the tourists photograph the fob-watch, then we went to Daimaru. We looked at some shavers, then went across the covered walkway to Myer to compare the prices. On the way we passed through the Myer shoe department: a large, low-ceilinged room filled with tables covered with red sheets and large piles of women's shoes. Shoppers stood around the tables like emergency medical staff attending to the dead and dying victims of some terrible disaster-movie catastrophe.

I said: 'I'm thinking about writing a story about Jackie Chan coming to Melbourne.'

My friend said: 'Haven't you written something like that before?'

I said: 'Yeah. Well, this time I'm writing about someone who isn't dead. I want to meet him. I want to ask him about the film and why he is setting it in New York. The narrator of the story will be kind of like me . . .'

My friend laughed.

I said: 'Yeah, all right. The narrator wants to meet Jackie Chan. After watching Jackie Chan filming he imagines that Jackie is performing some sort of transplant operation, turning Melbourne into New York. The narrator starts to feel like he is losing his sense of place. There are decisions you make when you decide to live somewhere, and then you have to decide whether your reasons for staying are better than the reasons for why you should try to live somewhere else. Either you stay and tell yourself that you have made the right decision or you move on, but once you start moving you may never stop.

'You look to the future. If you are successful there are more reasons to leave, to go somewhere you can capitalise on your success. That's what Jackie Chan is doing, setting his films in America so Americans will watch them. Then I think, what if the book is successful? I really feel like I belong here, but I'm never going to be able to make a living from writing if I stay here, and I can't keep working like this. There are plenty of reasons for me to leave, but in the process I would lose so much that is important to me. I only started writing after I moved to Melbourne, and all my friends are here, and I have more freedom here than I could have anywhere else. Now what is Jackie Chan going to do when the Chinese take over Hong Kong? What am I going to do now that the Liberals are in government? I feel like I have to decide, that somehow my situation and Jackie Chan's situation are linked, and whatever Jackie Chan decides, I'll abide by.'

My friend said: 'There's nothing new about what Jackie Chan is doing. Melbourne was based on a grid, like New York and all of the other cities either designed or redesigned during the Victorian era. Batman Hill, the only real distinguishing feature of the area, was flattened so all that remained was a level slope leading down to Swanston Street. The grid was there before there were any buildings: they had laid out wide streets before there was anything in them.

'The money to construct the buildings themselves was made during the goldrush, in places like Bendigo and Ballarat. They set about building a city that was not just well-off but educated and cultured. The aim was to build a cultured city, a European city. Throughout Melbourne they began reproducing not only the spirit of European enlightenment but also the physical things, the buildings themselves. There's a whole number of buildings which are copies of buildings in Europe and America, and the process has continued through to the present day. What Jackie Chan is doing makes sense, given that the history of Melbourne has been a constant process of imitation and reproduction anyway.'

In the end we both bought shavers. We both chose the same model, *twin* shavers, which was a little embarrassing. Then we drove back to the office and shaved.

The 'Duomo' of the Exhibition Buildings, Melbourne.

On Monday the job was finished and sent off to the client for approval. On Tuesday I slept in until lunchtime and then I called up a friend at the National Gallery. I rarely go to the National Gallery, and never to see the art. I caught the usual tram to the city, then I started walking along Swanston Street. Jackie Chan was filming on Swanston Street, between Collins and Bourke Streets. They had a truck with a camera mounted on the back tray. The truck was pulling a trailer, and in the trailer was an ornate white horse carriage. In New York, people hire carriages to take rides around Central Park. Someone in Melbourne copied the idea, taking tourists for rides around the city. Jackie Chan was lying on his back in the trailer, facing away from me. All I could see was the top of his head. A group of men dressed in grey suits stood behind the trailer. Some of their faces were familiar, the faces of extras from vaguely remembered Australian television shows.

I kept walking, over the Princess Bridge and down St Kilda Road until I reached the National Gallery. There is no saint called St Kilda: the name is a corruption of the Norse word *skildir*, meaning 'shields'. I read that somewhere. I entered through the exit door of the gallery. When I told the guard whom I had come to see he let me through. The gallery was empty except for a number of old women, either wandering alone or in pairs so they could hold each other up. The old women wore tweed jackets or furs and lots of scarves and impractically shaped hats.

I suppose they were the kind of old women you were meant to call old ladies. They wandered around the gallery, closely inspecting artworks which, even without the benefit of senility, I thought were incomprehensible. There were some works on show by a friend of mine, computer-generated images of potato-shaped, genetically-engineered human babies. An old woman was standing there, staring at the pictures with the expression of a religious martyr. I could not begin to imagine what the old woman was thinking. She probably wasn't thinking anything: either she was standing there for the length of time that politeness dictates a person should look at a work of art, or she was just getting her breath back. I felt like I was in the audience of some play by Jean-Paul Sartre set in Purgatory.

I made my way to the rear of the gallery, to the office where my friend worked. My friend was on the phone. While I waited for her to finish I looked in at the Members' Room next door, where old women chatted with each other, drank tea and ate biscuits, then reapplied their make-up and adjusted their hats before returning to their vigil, like the undead guardians of an ancestral tomb. Some of the old women still had living husbands who also came to the gallery, but the men never left the Members' Room. They just sat there and read the complimentary newspapers.

My friend and I went to have coffee in the gallery restaurant. I asked her if they had many deaths in the gallery, and she told me that an old woman had died during the Members' Light Luncheon the week before – turned blue and died between the main course and dessert.

I said: 'I want to write a story about Jackie Chan, but I don't know how to get in touch with him. I want to ask him some questions.'

She told me she would find out.

Then I said: 'I also want to know which buildings in Melbourne are copies. I need to make a list of them.'

She told me she had a friend who worked at the National Trust who knew all about the subject. She would arrange a meeting for me.

On the way back I passed the film crew again. The truck, with the carriage behind it, was being driven down Swanston Street. The extras in grey suits were running behind and Jackie Chan was hanging off one side of the carriage. In the carriage a woman was being held down by more extras in grey suits. At a given point Jackie would jump into the carriage and start fighting with the men in grey suits. Then the truck would be driven back to its starting position and the scene would be repeated. I stopped to watch for a long time.

The next few days I left the answering machine on and tried to catch up on some sleep. My friend from the gallery called up and left a message on the machine. I called her back, and she told me the phone number for Jackie Chan's publicist in Sydney, the fax number for Jackie Chan's production office in Hong Kong, and the name of a staff reporter at the *Herald Sun* who was in constant contact with the film crew – the intention being that if Jackie Chan was injured doing a stunt the reporter would be the first to get the story.

I said: 'How did you get all this information? How do you find out things like that?'

She said: 'It's my job.'

I told her I would wait to speak with her friend from the National Trust. I still didn't know if I had anything to write about, and I was expecting to have to do a few more days' work once my client got in touch with me about any changes that had to be made.

Once I had decided what I was going to say, I called the publicist's office in Sydney. I said: 'Hello. I'm a writer, and I'm doing a story about Jackie Chan. I need to get an interview with Jackie Chan. It's important.'

The woman I was speaking to told me that the bad weather had forced filming to run over schedule, so Jackie Chan was not doing any more interviews. She offered to send me a press release, which I got in the mail a few weeks later, but by then it no longer mattered. I put down the phone thinking I had no story after all.

I waited four weeks for the client to come back with a list of changes and corrections, four weeks that the work I had done sat, gathering dust, on somebody's desk. Then I got a call late on a Thursday afternoon, saying that they had made a list of changes that they needed by tomorrow morning. I told the girl that she would have to go to the office and sit there with me, all night if necessary, to approve each change as I made it. She told me she had other plans, but I refused to budge.

I call this my sleep-over policy. When clients have to sit with me all night, with nothing to do but make coffee for me and talk about themselves, a lot of the changes they wanted begin to look a lot less necessary than they had first thought, particularly when they see how long the work takes. I will also admit that, by this stage in the proceedings, making a difficult client suffer makes me feel good.

Just before I left for the office I got a phone call. I was invited to go out for dinner with some friends at Daimonji, a Japanese restaurant on the fourth floor of Melbourne Central. I wanted to go, but now I was committed to turning up at the office. If I sent the client home early so I could go out for dinner I would damage the credibility of my sleep-over policy if I had to use it again.

So I spent the night working, and the client spent the night talking. At one point she said: 'When you work in marketing it is important for your boss to tell you when you've done a good job. But sometimes my boss forgets to. See, in marketing you don't actually *do* anything, you just facilitate the work getting done. So the only way you can tell if you've done a good job is if the boss says you have.'

I told her I had the opposite problem.

Afterwards, my friends told me that Jackie Chan had been filming in the atrium of Melbourne Central that night. My friends left the restaurant late, after the rest of Melbourne Central had closed. They took the escalator down one floor, and from the balcony they could see a large crowd of people on the ground level of the atrium. The crowd, presumably hired extras, seemed very excited. My friends could see members of the film crew in their familiar yellow parkas but they didn't see Jackie Chan. Then a couple of security guards saw my friends and told them to keep moving.

This book will not be available in print until after the Chinese government has taken possession of Hong Kong. I would be foolish to speculate about what will (or has already) happened because I will most likely be wrong. Recording my speculations on these pages would be pointless.

But I imagine it will take a while longer for *A Nice Guy* to be released in theatres or on video. I know nothing about the content of the film, the details of the plot or the action that takes place, beyond the scenes and locations I have already described. The film could even be released with a different name. But now, when I go to Melbourne Central I cannot stop myself from imagining Jackie Chan being chased around the atrium of the shopping centre, jumping from one balcony to the next, running up and down the escalators and hanging, like a modern-day Harold Lloyd, from the hands of the over-sized Seiko fob-watch.

I saw the film crew one more time, on Spring Street at the Paris end of the city, in front of the statue of some civil servant, right by the Princess Theatre. I had been sent there on a job, setting up some work in a ground-floor office which looked out on the street where the filming was taking place.

The section of street had been blocked off at either end and filled with wrecked cars. Broken glass was everywhere, and the great crowd of spectators made the footpath nearly impassable. From inside the office I watched Samo Hung, the director, standing on the base of the statue and giving instructions, but I failed to see Jackie Chan at all. When I got home I called my friend at the National Gallery and arranged to meet her friend from the National Trust the next day.

She said: 'I heard that Jackie Chan has changed his mind about setting *A Nice Guy* in New York. It's going to be set in Melbourne after all. He just said: "Melbourne's a nice place. Why not set the film in Melbourne?"'

I forgot to bring my tape recorder to the meeting, so I made notes on a piece of paper. We met in an art gallery in the basement of a building near the corner of Collins and Swanston Streets. The building was designed in the 1900s to house an apothecary, but now it contained a hair salon, a beauty clinic, a travel agency and some other businesses as well as the gallery.

I asked him for a list of buildings that were copied from buildings in other cities.

He said: 'The dome of the Exhibition Building, one of the few remaining examples of the Victorian Exhibition movement, is based on the dome of the Florence Cathedral. The former Mint building is based on a Roman palazzo. Above the entrance of the Windsor Hotel are figures copied from the Medici Tomb by Leonardo. The Manchester Unity building has the turret of the Chicago Tribune building, while the new Telstra House is an exact copy of Walter Gropius's unsuccessful submission for the Chicago Tribune building competition. The Russell Street Police Station is a foreshortened version of the Empire State Building. The Princess Bridge, designed by Percy Grainger's father, is a copy of Black Friar's Bridge in London. The front pediment of the Shrine of Remembrance is copied from the Parthenon, and the stepped roof is copied from the tomb of Mausolus at Halicarnassus. The ICI Building is a copy of the Lever building in Chicago, and the BHP building is a copy of the ICI building.'

I walked up the stairs to the ground floor and out the front door and on to the street. I walked the short distance to Swanston Street and stood there facing the Manchester Unity building. I thought of a passage from Nathaneal West's *The Day of the Locust*:

He left the road and climbed across the spine of the hill to look down on the other side. From there he could see a ten-acre field of cockleburs spotted with clumps of sunflowers and wild gum. In the center of the field was a gigantic pile of sets, flats and props. While he watched, a ten-ton truck added another load to it. This was the final dumping ground. He thought of Janvier's 'Sargasso

Sea.' Just as that imaginary body of water was a history of civilization in the form of a marine junkyard, the studio lot was one in the form of a dream dump. A Sargasso of the imagination! And the dump grew continually, for there wasn't a dream afloat somewhere which wouldn't sooner or later turn up on it, having first been made photographic by plaster, canvas, lath and paint. Many boats sink and never reach the Sargasso, but no dream ever entirely disappears. Somewhere it troubles some unfortunate person and some day, when that person has been sufficiently troubled, it will be reproduced on the lot.

I knew what had made Jackie Chan change his mind.

The city of Melbourne had been pieced together like some gigantic stage set. That was why Jackie Chan had come, to work on the largest stage set in the world. But he had seen that Melbourne was also a city, **a gigantic living body** eighty kilometres across and filled with several million souls, not the dead studio lot of Nathaneal West's story.

I turned around and started walking. I took an hour or so to get back to the flat. I was in no hurry, and the weather was good. I walked up the stairs to the first floor with my keys in my hand. Someone had left the door to the hallway balcony open, and I looked out the door at the city skyline. The sight was the most beautiful sight I could imagine.

References

Books

Beck, Jerry and Friedwald, Will, *Looney Tunes and Merrie Melodies: a Complete Illustrated Guide to the Warner Bros. Cartoons*, Henry Holt & Company, 1989.

Chandler, Raymond, *The Chandler Collection*, 3 volumes, Picador, 1983.

De Landa, Manuel, *War in the Age of Intelligent Machines*, Swerve Editions, New York, 1991.

Diamond, Jared, *The Rise and Fall of the Third Chimpanzee*, Vintage, 1992.

Gogol, Nikolai, *Diary of a Madman and Other Stories*, trans. Ronald Wilks, Penguin, 1972.

Hersey, George, *The Lost Meaning of Classical Architecture*, MIT Press, 1988.

Hoffmann, E.T.A., *Tales of Hoffmann*, trans. R.J. Hollingdale, Penguin, 1982.

Hofstadter, Douglas, *Metamagical Themas*, Basic Books, 1985.

Jane's Spacecraft

Knight, Bernard, *The Post-Mortem Technician's Handbook: A Manual of Mortuary Practice*, Blackwell Scientific Publications, 1984.

Paré, Ambroise, *Of Monsters and Marvels (Des Monstres et prodiges)*.

——, *The Case Reports and Autopsy Records of Ambroise Paré*.

Plueckhahn, Vernon D., *Lectures on Forensic Medicine and Pathology*, University of Melbourne Printing Services, Department of Pathology, 1976.

Poe, Edgar Allan, *The Fall of the House of Usher and Other Writings*, Penguin, 1986.

Regis, Ed, *Great Mambo Chicken and the Transhuman Condition: Science Slightly Over the Edge*, Addison-Wesley, 1990.

Roussel, Raymond, *Life, Death and Works: Atlas Anthology 4*, Atlas Press, 1987.

———, *Locus Solus*, trans. Rupert Copeland Cuningham, Calder & Boyars, 1970.

Savinio, Alberto, *The Lives of the Gods*, Atlas Press, 1991.

Stern, Jane and Michael, *Encyclopedia of Bad Taste*, HarperPerennial, 1990.

———, *Encyclopedia of Pop Culture*, HarperPerennial, 1992.

Sterne, Laurence, *The Life and Opinions of Tristram Shandy*, Penguin, 1967.

Thompson, C. J. S., *The Mystery and Lore of Monsters*, University Books, 1968.

Weldon, Michael J., *Psychotronic Encyclopedia of Film*, Ballantine Books, 1983.

———, *Psychotronic Video Guide*, St Martin's, Griffin Edition, 1996.

West, Nathaneal, *The Day of the Locust*, New Directions Publishing, 1962.

Wilkins, Mike, Doug Kirby and Ken Smith, *New Roadside America*, Simon & Shuster, 1992

Movies

The 5000 Fingers of Dr T, Columbia, 1953, script by Doctor Seuss and Alan Scott

The Thing with Two Heads, American International Pictures, 1972.

Forbidden Planet, MGM, 1956.

The Good, the Bad and the Ugly, United Artists, 1966.

Early to Bet, Warner Brothers, 1951.

The Night of the Hunter, MGM, 1955.

Bring Me the Head of Alfredo Garcia, MGM, 1974.

The Raymond Scott Archives

Chairmen Of The Preservation Committee:
Irwin Chusid
Mark Mothersbaugh
Mr Bonzai

Advisory Board:
Gert-Jan Blom, The Beau Hunks
Don Byron
Bob Camp, the *Ren & Stimpy Show*
Will Friedwald
David Garland
David Harrington, Kronos Quartet
Lee Herschberg
Dick Hyman
Leonard Maltin
Robert Moog, Moog Music, Inc.
Andy Partridge, XTC
Henry Rollins
Piet Schreuders
David M. Schwartz
Paul Verna
Hal Willner

The Raymond Scott Archives

Raymond Scott's private collection of recordings was donated by Mrs. Scott to the Marr Archives Sound Archives at the University of Missouri in 1994. The Marr Archives is undertaking a major preservation and restoration project on the collection, which includes 2,719 discs (from 1932 to the late 1950s), 602 open reel tapes, and various Scott papers, photos and memorabilia.

The Marr Archives estimates the project will cost about US$46,000. Some of that money will come from the University, but the remainder must come from private donations.

The Marr Archives is taking an inventory of the collection and compiling a preliminary documentation of titles, personnel, sessions, and dates. The discs will be cleaned just prior to being re-recorded on open reel tape (which will require the services of an engineer) for archival preservation. Eventually, the Marr Archives hopes to catalog the entire collection and put it on a national database so scholars, researchers and music buffs will have access to the material.

The collection is now owned by the Marr Archives, but commercial rights belong to the Scott estate. This will ensure that there will be more albums of Raymond Scott's music released in the future.

The value of this collection is incalculable; it constitutes over a half-century of music history, from the dawn of the Swing Era to the age of MIDI. The collection includes recordings of the Raymond Scott Quintette and Orchestras, and collaborations with Charlie Shavers, Ben Webster, Frank Sinatra, Dorothy Collins, Bo Diddley, Mel Torme,

Jim Henson, Paul Whiteman, Cozy Cole, Gloria Lynne and others. The tapes reflect Scott's pioneering work with homemade electronic sequencers, synthesizers, the Clavivox (keyboard theremin) and the Electronium (his 'instantaneous composition/performance machine').

All U.S. financial donations are 501(c)3 tax-deductible.
Cheques should be payable to: The University of Missouri, Kansas City.
Mark on your cheque:
For Raymond Scott Collection
and send to:
Dr Ted Sheldon
University of Missouri at Kansas City
Miller Nichols Library
Kansas City, MO 64110-2499

We hope you appreciate the worthiness of the project, and that we can count on your support.

PENGUIN – THE BEST AUSTRALIAN READING

Running Backwards Over Sand   Stephanie Dowrick

Zoë Delighty had to start from the beginning and piece herself together again ...

Her mother's early death marked a turning point in her young life. It was as though everything she adored and trusted died with her. Zoë's imaginative life becomes her greatest strength, and the catalyst for her escape.

Like her compatriot Katherine Mansfield before her, Zoë flees to Europe – to London and Berlin. She lives a colourful, even dazzling life. But fleeing the past does not erase it. Her journey through friendships, lovers of both sexes, literature, sexual politics and changing external landscapes must continue until, making peace with her ghosts, she can find peace within herself.

PENGUIN – THE BEST AUSTRALIAN READING

Sapphires Sara Dowse

'Security is an illusion, Evelyn. Life is a precarious business. The best approach is to learn to like it that way.'

Evelyn Hazelwood is the descendant of the Kozminsky clan. Her grandmother fled as a child from Tsarist Russia to the American plains; her mother was drawn to the glitter of the city. Evelyn's own flight takes her to Sydney, where she ends up making a living of sorts writing comedy sketches for television. Her family's wanderings are a mini-diaspora that moves from century to century and halfway across the world. One day, Evelyn stops running long enough to plumb the meaning of her past.

Drawing on the tradition of Yiddish storytelling, Sara Dowse shapes a new vision of the vexatious destiny of Jewish women. With the lightest of touches, she explores the links between the generations in a passionate, humorous and profound work of fiction.

PENGUIN – THE BEST AUSTRALIAN READING

Cosmo Cosmolino Helen Garner

What sort of a household can three lost souls create?

Janet, a sharp-tongued sceptic washed up from the seventies; Ray, a moth-eaten, haunted fundamentalist; and Maxine, driven, shameless, ecstatic about auras and angels – in Janet's run-down house they slug it out, blundering across each other's secret pasts, until Maxine, in her hilarious innocence, bursts the barricade between dream and reality, and blasts a path into the future.

PENGUIN – THE BEST AUSTRALIAN READING

The Orchard Thieves Elizabeth Jolley

'If you have the house,' the middle sister said to the aunt, the eldest sister, '. . . you'll have to pay us each one-third of the current market price . . .'

Every household is haunted by times of discord which destroy the wished-for calm. Every number of a family feels that their own difficulties are unique.

The grandmother, mother of three grown-up daughters, understands that it is the unseen, the unspoken and the unrevealed which either perplex or console people in their family dealings.

When the middle sister returns home from England, without any explanations about her private life, peace in the grandmother's house is jeopardised. The grandmother, with imagination, acceptance and the quality of her affection, attempts a form of rescue in the face of rising conflict and tension.

The Well Elizabeth Jolley

One night Miss Hester Harper and Katherine are driving home from a celebration, a party at a hotel in town, when, in the deadly still countryside, they knock something down. It's a man, whose body they proceed to dump, with great difficulty, in a farmyard well. The next morning cries are heard coming from the bottom of the well . . . An extraordinary, original novel with Elizabeth Jolley's usual potent mixture of scarcely suppressed violence and eroticism.

PENGUIN – THE BEST AUSTRALIAN READING

The Penguin Leunig   Michael Leunig

Leunig's subjects are as ambitious as his technique is simple. World cataclysm, the Flood, loneliness, cruelty, lust and greed ... Sometimes whimsical, this prodigiously gifted artist is never guilty of whimsy, and, mercifully, he is never 'relevant', 'socially aware' or 'narrowly political'.

The Travelling Leunig   Michael Leunig

Another collection of Leunig's mad and magical excursions into the absurdities of life.

PENGUIN – THE BEST AUSTRALIAN READING

More, Please Barry Humphries

The details of Barry Humphries' life are still amongst the best kept secrets of our time. Recent volumes devoted to his work and career shed very little, if any, light on this most private and circumspect of artistes. Hitherto, he has deliberately furnished his hardworking biographers with blatant mystifications and whimsical fictions.

In consequence the revelations and confessions contained in this book will astonish his growing international public with their novelty and in no way echo the amiable, but wildly inaccurate, narratives of his recent memorialists. Here, at last, and in his own lapidary prose, is his account of his life up to the present.

More, Please was his first utterance and they are the two words that will inevitably spring to the lips of all those who read this book.

PENGUIN – THE BEST AUSTRALIAN READING

The Kadaitcha Sung Sam Watson

In his twentieth year, mixed-blood Aborigine Tommy Gubba is initiated in the eternal flames into an ancient clan of sorcerers – the Kadaitcha. He is sent into the mortal world to take revenge on the fair-skinned race who have plundered its wealth and laid waste to the chosen people. His fate has been ordained, and Tommy must race against time to confront a savage, evil foe.

PENGUIN – THE BEST AUSTRALIAN READING

The Penguin Best Australian Short Stories Edited by Mary Lord

What sort of stories do Australian writers tell?

Set in cities, in suburbia, and in the outback, Mary Lord's selection of short stories explores the subtleties, the humour and the sadness of human life. For anyone interested in Australian writing and the changing views of Australian writers this is an essential collection.

John George Lang
Marcus Clarke
Edward Dyson
John Arthur Barry
Henry Lawson
Katharine Susannah Prichard
Marjorie Barnard
Hal Porter
Christina Stead
Elizabeth Jolley
Morris Lurie
Helen Garner
Frank Moorhouse
Janette Turner Hospital

Mary Fortune
Jessie Couvreur
William Astley
Steele Rudd
Barbara Baynton
Henry Handel Richardson
Patrick White
John Morrison
Michael Wilding
Peter Carey
Olga Masters
Beverley Farmer
Tim Winton
Marion Halligan